MORE *Bloody* HOROWITZ

WALKER
BOOKS

For Cassian –
with thanks for the title

This is a work of fiction. Names, characters, places and
incidents are either the product of the author's imagination or,
if real, are used fictitiously. All statements, activities, stunts,
descriptions, information and material of any other kind
contained herein are included for entertainment purposes only
and should not be relied on for accuracy or replicated as they
may result in injury.

First published 2010 by Walker Books Ltd
87 Vauxhall Walk, London SE11 5HJ

10 9 8 7 6 5 4 3 2 1

This book has been typeset in Bookman and Goudy Old Style.

Printed in Italy

British Library Cataloguing in Publication Data:
a catalogue record for this book is available
from the British Library

ISBN 978-1-4063-1700-8

www.walker.co.uk

www.anthonyhorowitz.com

CONTENTS

Darren Shan had come for him...

THE MAN WHO KILLED DARREN SHAN

LOOKING BACK, HENRY PARKER could honestly say that he had never wanted to hurt anyone. Certainly, it had never occurred to him that he would one day plan and then execute the perfect murder of an internationally well-known children's author … even if that was what actually happened. To begin with, all Henry wanted to do was write.

Even as a boy he had dreamed of being a writer. No, not just a writer, but an Author with a capital A – published, with a fan club, his book in every bookshop window, his photograph in the Sunday newspapers and a great pile of money in the bank. And what sort of writing would make his name and put that name on the front of a million books?

Henry loved horror. To him, the only good story was one that had people dying, knives cutting into flesh, brains exploding and blood dripping from every paragraph. In "Verbal Abuse", written when he was just sixteen years old and still at school, a boy was actually crucified by his Latin teacher for talking in class, while in another work, "Tooth Decay", a Birmingham dentist was torn to shreds by one of his patients who turned out to be a werewolf.

Having written these stories, Henry wasn't sure who to show them to. His wealthy parents were abroad most of the time and didn't seem to have a lot of interest in their only son. He didn't really have any friends. In the end, he went to his English teacher and asked him to look at the neatly-bound manuscript he'd carried to school in his backpack. "I'd be very grateful if you would tell me what you think, sir," he said. "Although, personally, I think they're very good."

The teacher, Mr Harris, accepted the task with pleasure. He was always glad when any of his young students showed initiative in this way. However, after reading the pages at home, he wasn't quite so sure. "Your work does show promise, Henry," he muttered. "But I have to say, I did find some of your writing a little … over the top."

"What do you mean, sir?" Henry asked.

"Well, do you really have to be quite so explicit? This paragraph here – where the dentist's heart is pulled out and then minced – I read it after dinner and felt quite ill."

"But it's a werewolf!" Henry protested.

"Werewolves enjoy mincing human organs."

"And in this other story … the boy being nailed down in that way. Wouldn't it have been better to leave a little to the imagination?"

"My readers may not have any imagination," Henry replied.

"I'm sure that's not true." Mr Harris sighed. "Have you considered writing any other genre? Romance, for example. Or perhaps a spy story?"

"I prefer horror."

"Well, I don't want to discourage you. It's very good to see you taking an interest in anything at all. But I don't think you're going to succeed unless you tone it down a little. Scaring people is one thing, but making them feel sick is quite another."

That night, Henry began a new story in which a stupid English teacher called Mr Harris was captured by cannibals and eaten alive.

Two years went by. Inevitably, Henry wrote less as his A-levels took over his life. He did not get brilliant results, managing only two Cs and a D. His worst marks were for English Literature. In one paper he wrote five hundred words describing the murder of Duncan in Shakespeare's *Macbeth*; the woman who marked it actually resigned from the examinations board the very next day.

Henry didn't go to university. By the time he left school, he felt he had learned more than enough and that three more years of education would only get in the way of his becoming a world-famous author. His parents owned a large house in Reading where he could live. He was fairly sure that his father would support him while he wrote his first full-length novel. He already had the beginnings of an idea. Fame and fortune were surely only just round the corner.

But then two things happened that changed everything. First of all his parents died in a bizarre accident. They had gone to a circus outside Munich – Henry's mother had always been fond of trapeze artists – and they'd been having a wonderful time until the turn had come for the human cannonball to perform. Something had gone wrong. Instead of being fired into the safety net, the human cannonball had been blasted, with some force, into the third row of the stalls, killing Mr and Mrs Parker instantly.

The second disaster was that Henry discovered that his parents had left him no money at all. In fact, it was even worse than that. In recent years, their business (in dental equipment) had taken a distinct downturn and their borrowing had got so out of hand that their home and all their possessions had to be sold off to pay their debts. And so, at just nineteen, Henry found himself broke and alone.

Somehow, he needed to earn a living. With such poor A-levels that wasn't going to be easy, but a friend of his parents' took pity on him and managed to get him a job as an estate agent. This involved showing people around properties in Battersea, south London – and he hated it. He sneered at the other estate agents and he was jealous of the young couples moving into houses and flats that he himself couldn't possibly afford. He was now renting a single room that backed onto the main railway line from Victoria Station.

But he still had his dream. More than that, he had the use of a desk, paper and pens, and the office computer. And so, every evening when the agency closed, he would stay behind, tapping away into the small hours. He was writing his novel. Two thousand words a night, five nights a week – Henry figured it would be finished in less than three months.

In fact it took him eleven years.

Writing is a strange business. You write a sentence and then you read it and one word leaps out at you. Or should that be *jumps* out at you? Or *bothers* you? And then you go over

and over it, and by the evening you find you haven't written two thousand words at all. You've only managed a couple of sentences, and even they don't strike you as being quite right. So you start again and again, crossing out and crumpling the pages into balls, and no matter how hard you try you never quite reach the two words you're most keen to write: THE END.

That was how it was for Henry. Eleven long years of showing people around properties, working through the night and sleeping right through the weekends certainly took their toll. By the time he was thirty, he had lost most of his hair and much of his eyesight. He wore thick glasses and sat with a stooped back. A poor diet and lack of exercise had both hollowed him and drained much of the colour from his skin. The honest truth was that if he had gone to a funeral, no one would have known whether he was the undertaker or the corpse.

But at last he finished the novel. And reading it through while chewing on a cheese rind – which was all he had been able to find in the fridge – he knew he had created a masterpiece. A horror novel for children, one hundred thousand words long and like nothing anyone had ever written before.

Curiously, it was the death of his parents that had inspired him. Although he had been shocked by their sudden end, and even more by the disappearance of their wealth, Henry had never really missed them. His father had always been bad-tempered and his mother too busy to look after him. But the way they had died had given him the idea of writing a story that would begin in a circus; not an ordinary circus, but a world inhabited by strange creatures ... freaks.

His novel was called *Ring of Evil* and told the story of a young boy who ran away from home and got a job in the circus, only to find himself surrounded by ghosts, werewolves, witches and vampires. Henry described in loving detail how the vampires would chase members of the audience into the car park, tear their throats open and drink their blood. The hero's name was Justin and in chapter five he was turned into a vampire himself. He then spent chapters six, seven and eight killing people, gradually discovering that being a vampire was fun … certainly more fun than being a schoolboy. Eventually, Justin teamed up with the ringmaster – who was called Mephisto and who turned out to be the son of Count Dracula himself – and the two of them set off on an adventure that brought them into contact with two vampire armies, fighting for control of the world.

The final chapter was set in New York City, and finished with the whole of Fifth Avenue turning into a river of blood. At least a thousand people were killed as the two vampire armies joined battle in the subway system. Mephisto himself was impaled on a metal spike (the description ran to three paragraphs) and Justin returned to England and took over the circus.

THE END.

Henry typed the words in bold and underlined them twice.

That evening he left the office at the same time as everyone else and bought himself a half-bottle of champagne which he sipped, on his own, in his room as the trains rumbled past outside. He had spent twenty pounds having the manuscript photocopied and bound, and he couldn't stop himself flicking through the pages, running his hands over the cover, reading his favourite paragraphs again and again. He had absolutely no doubt that *Ring of Evil* would be a huge, international success. He went to bed that night working on the speech that he would make when he won the Carnegie Medal, which was only awarded to the very greatest writers. The book was everything he had hoped it would be … and more.

The next day he put the manuscript into an envelope and sent it to one of the most famous publishers in London. He had noticed their name on a number of bestsellers and guessed they must know a thing or two about children's fiction. Three days later, he received a polite note, thanking him for the manuscript and assuring him that the publisher would contact him shortly.

The next month was a nightmare. Henry was in such a state of nervous excitement that he couldn't eat or sleep. When he showed customers around flats, all he could think of was blood and vampires, book signings and VIP travel around the world. The next month was just as bad. By the third month he was beginning to wonder just how long the famous publisher needed to read one hundred thousand words.

And then the letter came.

Dear Mr Barker…

It was a bad start. They hadn't even got his name right.

Thank you for sending us your novel, Ring of Evil. *Although your work shows a great deal of imagination and energy, I regret to say that I do not think it is suitable for publication.*

You say that this is a work for children but I would be very concerned, personally, by the levels of violence and bloodshed. I think you would find that most teachers and librarians would not want this on their shelves. At the same time, the book is clearly not adult enough – particularly with a hero who is only twelve.

I'm afraid, therefore, that I am returning the manuscript. I hope you won't be too discouraged and wish you luck elsewhere.

Yours sincerely,

Hilary Spurling – Senior Editor

Henry read the letter once. Then he read it again. He felt a rush of different emotions. The first was disbelief. *Ring of Evil* had been rejected! Disbelief was followed by dismay. All those hours of work, the weeks and the months – for nothing! Then came anger. Who was Hilary Spurling? What did she know? How could she be so shallow and arrogant, to dismiss his one-hundred-thousand-word manuscript with a letter that didn't even reach much more than dozen lines? Muttering a curse, Henry reached for a second envelope. There were plenty of publishers in London. A few weeks from now, Hilary Spurling would be weeping bitter tears. And she would be a senior editor no longer, fired from her job for missing the biggest bestseller of the decade when it had been sitting right there in her hands.

In the next twelve months, *Ring of Evil* was rejected by another eight London publishers as well as three literary agents. By now, Henry had left the estate agency. Everyone in the office knew that he'd been writing a novel and he couldn't bear to tell them that he hadn't managed to sell it. He got a job in a warehouse in Shoreditch, supplying chemicals to laboratories around London. There was no computer there for him to work on after hours. But nor did he want one. If his first book – his masterpiece – wasn't going to be published, why should he even think about writing a second?

And that might have been the end of it. Henry could have ended his days bitter and defeated, unhappy, unmarried and alone. Perhaps he'd have been found in the corner of his local pub, propping up the bar with one whisky too many, dreaming of what might have been. He could have worked at the warehouse until he retired and then, after a couple of years in a dreary old people's home, quietly died.

But everything changed one day when he walked into a bookshop near Victoria Station. He hadn't even gone in to buy a book. He had just needed somewhere to shelter from a storm. But while he was inside, waiting for the rain to die down, his eye was caught by a pile of books on the front table. Puzzled, he picked one up. The book was called *Cirque du Freak* and it was written by someone called Darren Shan.

The back cover told him everything he needed to know. The hero was a boy called Darren Shan – it was strange that he had the same name as the author – who sneaked away from home to visit a travelling freak show. Henry flicked through the pages. The book struck him as very short. Every chapter was topped with a picture of a skull. Before he had even left the shop, he had got the general idea of the story. Darren Shan's best friend was bitten by a spider, and in order to save him Darren had to become a vampire and…

It was *his* story! There could be no doubt about it. Of course, not all the ideas were the same. But the circus, the freaks, the vampires, the child hero, even some of the names were too similar for it to be pure coincidence. For example, in Shan's book there was a character called Mr Crepsley – almost the same name as one of the clowns (Mr Crispy) in Henry's. Shan's best friend was called Steve. In *Ring of Evil* a character called Steve was murdered in chapter twenty-seven. Henry looked at the cover. As he gazed at the name of the publisher, a black fury rose up inside him. The same publisher had turned down *Ring of Evil*.

He bought the book and took it home, and that night he spent several hours reading *Cirque du Freak*, underlining passages in red and circling words. As the sun rose, he was one hundred per cent certain. The publisher had taken his manuscript and given it to another author. This author – Darren Shan – had copied the best bits and published the book as his own. He had stolen the result of eleven years' work!

And to make things worse, Shan was getting brilliant reviews. The next morning Henry rang in to say he would be late for work. He scuttled off to an internet café down the road and Googled everything he could about *Cirque du Freak*. The critics were unanimous. Here was a well-crafted and completely original story which would attract even the most unwilling readers. Another fourteen volumes planned, and publishers were snapping them up all around the world. A major Hollywood film was on the way. Overnight, Darren Shan had become a star.

Henry went straight back to his room, sat down and composed a letter, writing with a pen that kept leaking ink, in jagged handwriting that lay on the page like dead spiders.

"Dear Mr Shan," he began.

I have just read your book, "Cirque du Freak" and have noticed many similarities to a book of mine, "Ring of Evil". My book is set in a circus, just like yours. My book has vampires in it, just like yours. My book also has a boy hero who is only two years younger than yours. And I could point to several phrases in your book that also appear in mine. For example, on page 33, you say, "It was Friday evening, the end of the school week..." Almost exactly the same words – though in a different order – appear on page 297 of my manuscript! Again, on page 124, you describe your teeth as "clattering". That description is obviously taken from page 311 of my book which describes window shutters in exactly the same way.

I could give you a hundred more examples.

I would like to know who it was at your publisher who showed you my manuscript and whose idea it was to steal it and make it your own. We will discuss how much money you should pay me later.

Yours sincerely,

Henry Parker

It took three weeks for Henry to receive a reply, and when it came it wasn't from Darren Shan at all. It was from someone called Fenella Jones who worked at the publishing house. It read:

Dear Mr Parker,

Thank you for your letter. I can assure you that Cirque du Freak *is a completely original piece of work. Mr Shan wrote it without any discussion with us and we are very proud to have published it.*

I am sorry if you feel that there are similarities to your own book.

With best wishes,

Fenella Jones – Editorial Assistant

And that was it. No apology. No explanation. No promise of money. Just a few lines dismissing him as if he would simply crawl away and forget the whole thing.

Over the next six months, Henry wrote nine more letters, and when *The Vampire's Assistant*, the second book in the series, was published and was even more successful than the first, he wrote eleven more. He got no reply to any of them. It seemed that Darren Shan and his publishers had decided to pretend he didn't exist.

As The Saga of Darren Shan grew and became ever more popular, Henry bought all the books and went through each one, not once but several times, making notes in a pile of exercise books that he kept by his bed. Of course, it was easy enough to convince himself that certain words and phrases had been copied from his novel, and even when the saga went off in a completely different direction from *Ring of Evil* he was able to persuade himself that Shan had changed his plans because he was afraid of being sued. Or maybe now he was stealing his ideas from somebody else.

At the same time, Henry began to collect as much information as he could about Darren Shan. He learned that the writer was surprisingly young and lived in Northern Ireland. He cut out pictures of him from newspapers. Shan was short and stocky, with closely cut hair and a face that was as round as a pumpkin. Henry thought he looked more like a footballer than a professional author. It seemed he had once worked as a teacher. He visited Shan's website and began to follow his progress through Britain and around the world. It soon became clear that there wasn't a country on the planet where the books weren't doing well. And all the time Henry could feel jealousy, like a cancer, creeping through him. *Cirque du Freak* was *his* book. It was *his* idea. *He* should have been the one enjoying the fame, the wealth, the jet-setting life.

Henry would never be able to remember the exact moment when he decided to murder Darren Shan. It wasn't an idea that simply arrived – a sudden inspiration. It was more like a growing awareness that murder was the only answer. He wanted to punish the successful writer. But more than that, he needed to get rid of him, to stop him existing. As far as Henry could see, it was the only way to allow his own life to continue. Without Shan, there would be no more books in the *Cirque du Freak* series. And then, just possibly, there might be room for *Ring of Evil*. But the truth was, Henry no longer cared whether his own novel was published or not. He had

fallen into a quicksand of hatred and despair. He wanted to lash out one last time before he was sucked under completely.

But how to do it?

Shan made occasional appearances in London where he would sign books for long queues of his devoted readers. It would be easy enough for Henry to join the line with some sharp implement concealed beneath his jacket. That would be appropriate. There was plenty of blood in Shan's books already. Henry would add a few pints more.

But despite everything, he didn't want to go to prison. It wouldn't be fair. After all, he was the victim here and he would only be giving Shan what he deserved. And he certainly didn't want to spend the rest of his life surrounded by common criminals. Henry thought about it and decided. He was an artist. He would use his talents to commit the perfect murder. And one day, maybe, he would write about it. Yes. He would have to change a few names and places, but killing Darren Shan might actually make a good subject for a book.

It wasn't going to be easy. Henry had to kill someone he had never met before – and probably never would meet. He had to do it from a distance. Yes. That was it. Almost at once an idea began to take shape in his mind.

Like many successful authors, Shan received fan letters and mentioned on his website that he tried to reply to as many as possible. Henry had already written to him once and had received a reply from some editorial assistant. But suppose he were to write again, pretending to be a twelve-year-old boy…? Shan would have to write back. And that would be it. It would be easy. Nobody would ever be able to pin anything on Henry.

The very next day, Henry stole a pair of rubber gloves from work – the sort used to protect workers' hands from dangerous chemicals. He would need them to make sure he didn't leave any fingerprints. He bought a cheap pen and some writing paper – choosing a common brand. Then he sat down and composed his letter.

"Dear Mr Shan," he began. He was careful to disguise his writing. He used large, looping letters to make it look as if the letter had been written by a young boy.

I am a huge fan of your work. I think you are a great writer. I have read all your books but my favourite was Vampire Mountain which I thought was briliant.

He misspelled brilliant on purpose. He was meant to be a schoolboy.

I would be very grateful if you could send me an autograph. I know you are busy so I am enclosing a stamped addressed envelope. Right now I am in hospital and the doctors are very worried about me. So your autograph means a lot to me. Please send it soon.

Yours sincerely,

Steve Lyons

He signed the letter with a fake name – in fact it was based on the character Steve Leopard he had read about in Shan's book. He was particularly pleased with the lie about being in hospital. It made it doubly certain that he would get a response. But the most brilliant – or briliant – part came next. With his work in the Shoreditch warehouse, Henry regularly came into contact with poisons and dangerous chemicals. It wasn't all that difficult to steal a small phial of liquid that was colourless, odourless and totally lethal. He mixed this with glue and then, using a paintbrush, applied it to the inside flap of an envelope which he addressed to

Steve Lyons at a false address in Brighton.

The trap was simple. Shan would read the letter asking for his autograph. He would sign his name on a card and slip it into the stamped addressed envelope. And when he licked the flap, he would seal his fate. Henry reckoned he would be dead before he reached the nearest post box, and with a bit of luck the police wouldn't even be able to work out how the poison had been administered.

Finally, just to be on the safe side, Henry took a train to Brighton and posted the deadly letter there. With no fingerprints, a false name and no misleading postcode on the stamp, he was confident that nobody would ever trace the letter back to him.

He sat back and waited. The next few days passed with a sense of continual excitement … almost, in fact, like reading a good book. Every evening he hurried home to his single room to catch the seven o'clock news on his television, the picture flickering each time a train went past. He couldn't wait to hear it… "And after the break, the children's author who took a tumble. Darren Shan's painful end…"

But in fact it was the newspapers that gave him the story he most wanted to hear. It was as he was leaving the warehouse, on his way to Shoreditch station, that he saw the words in bold type, hanging on the side of the kiosk:

CHILDREN'S AUTHOR MURDERED

Just three words – but the most brilliant phrase Henry had ever read. He fumbled in his pocket for cash and bought the paper and there it was, on the front page.

POLICE SUSPECT "POISON-PEN LETTER"

Darren Shan, the moderately popular children's author, died shortly after being admitted to hospital this morning. Shan, 32, had been answering his fan mail when he was suddenly taken ill. His assistant, Fenella Jones, called an ambulance but despite their best efforts, paramedics were unable to revive him.

Shan, whose Cirque du Freak series has topped bestseller lists all over the world, was in the middle of a second series known as The Demonata, and fans have already begun a candle-lit vigil outside his Dublin home. At first it was believed that he had succumbed to an attack of food poisoning, but police are now examining mail that he received in the morning post. Detective Superintendent John Dervish said, "It is possible that Mr Shan was the victim of a fan – or a madman pretending to be a fan. At the moment we are looking at every possibility."

The story went on over the page and there was a picture of Shan signing books, surrounded by children. Henry read the report with a mixture of emotions. Of course, he was delighted that his plan had succeeded. But at the same time, he was a little nervous that the police had so quickly figured out the murder method – the poison-pen letter, as the newspaper had put it. In a way, he was glad – he wanted the world to know that the writer had been punished, not just struck down by a piece of bad chicken or fish. But if the police had found out this much, this quickly, might their investigation lead them to him? No. Neither the paper nor the envelope could be traced to him. The letter had been postmarked Brighton, which was miles away. He had been careful to avoid leaving fingerprints. And even the poison that he had used was fairly common. Plenty of people could have got hold of it.

Henry watched the seven o'clock news with a growing sense of confidence. He watched the news again at ten o'clock, and at eleven o'clock, and each time the report was the same. The death of the young writer was a tragedy. The police were looking into it. But so far they had no clues, nothing to report.

Henry went to bed that night, fairly certain that he had got away with it. It didn't even occur to him that he had taken a human life, that he would have left behind a grieving family ... not to mention several thousand fans. As far as he was concerned, what he had done had been well executed. Nothing more, nothing less. It was as if the murder were a story that he had plotted, and it certainly had an utterly happy end.

It was the end of November and the weather had recently turned cold. There was only one radiator in Henry's room and although it was turned on full, it never seemed to give out much heat. The window frame was cracked, and some nights the wood rattled and cold breezes danced around the room. This was just such a night. More than that, a mist seemed to have risen around Victoria. There was a full moon but it seemed pale and yellow, unable to penetrate the cloud.

Henry tried to sleep but he couldn't. Though he pulled the duvet over his head, the chill still got in. He could feel it around his neck, creeping down his spine. His room was always a little damp and tonight he could almost see the moisture glistening on the walls. He was annoyed with himself. This was supposed to be his night of triumph. Maybe he should have gone out and bought himself a drink ... or several. He had committed a murder and got away with it! Surely that was something to celebrate.

"Henry…" The voice came as a whisper out of the darkness.

He had dreamed it, of course. It was a ghost voice, like something in a horror film, rising up from a swamp or out of a ruined castle. Only … how could he have dreamed it when he wasn't yet asleep?

"Henry…" The whisper came again, louder this time and filled with venom.

Henry hunched himself up in bed, drawing his knees to his chest, looking around him. There was a strange, green glow outside his window. His room looked out onto a strip of wasteland with the railway just beyond. Normally, he could see walls covered with graffiti and topped with broken glass and barbed wire. But the mist had grown thicker. It had smothered the outside world. And as he watched, wide-eyed, he saw it trickling under his door, filling the very room where he lay.

"Who is it?" he whimpered. The door crashed open. It seemed to have torn itself out of the frame – for there was nobody on the other side. More mist rolled in, and Henry smelled something thick and horrible, like dead, decaying meat. At the same time he heard footsteps, echoing along the corridor. He wondered what had happened to his landlady. She had a room on the floor above and must surely have heard all this. He tried to call out her name but his throat had seized up. He was petrified. No words came.

A figure formed in the half-light, then stepped into the room.

Henry stared. He raised a hand, his fingers twisted as if broken, like an animal claw. He knew what he was seeing. He couldn't believe it. But he had to accept it.

Darren Shan had come for him.

The children's writer had been dead for at least twenty-four hours. His skin was a hideous shade of white – it was obvious that not a drop of blood was being pumped through his veins. His eyes were also white and lifeless, as if covered in cataracts. At some point, blood must have gushed out of his mouth and over his chin for it was still there, dried now, a horrible, dark brown stain. His clothes were stiff with it. He was wearing a strange nightgown – but Henry recognized what it was. A shroud. He would have been wearing it in his coffin.

How could it be happening? Henry was trembling so hard he was making the bed shake. Tears of sheer terror were trickling down his face. At the same time, a terrible thought was working its way through his mind. Darren Shan was a horror writer. In *Cirque du Freak* he had even claimed to be a semi-vampire. Well, suppose it was true? Suppose he was, in some way, in touch with dark forces, with the ghosts and the monsters that inspired him? Shan was dead. Henry had seen it on the television and read it in the newspapers. And now he had come back from the grave, continuing his life's work even after that life had ended.

"You killed me," the creature rasped, his voice rattling in his throat. And as he spoke, Henry saw that his tongue had gone green and there was some dark-coloured liquid dribbling over his lower lip.

"No!" Henry replied. He wiped away his tears, but more instantly followed. "How did you find me?" he whimpered. "How did you get here?"

"You wrote to me." Darren Shan shuddered. "You made me reply. And when I licked the envelope … the pain! It was you, Henry Parker."

"Go away! Just go away!" Henry closed his eyes, hoping this was just some sort of hallucination. But when he opened them again, Shan was still there. "You stole my idea!" Henry screeched. He couldn't help himself. And at the same time, he had a sudden, crazy thought. This could hardly be better. He had spent months and months waiting to tell Darren Shan what he thought of him. Well, now Shan had returned from the grave to hear it. What was he going to do about it? He was a phantom! If he wanted to contact the police, he'd have to do it with a Ouija board. "You stole *Ring of Evil* from me. I sent it to your publisher and they gave it to you. You took my story and my characters and you made millions of pounds and I got nothing. Well, now I've shown you. I came up with the perfect murder. Yours! And soon you'll be forgotten but I'll write another book and nothing will stop me…"

"You killed me!" Shan wailed.

"Yes, I did. It was so easy. A little potassium cyanide mixed with the glue on the envelope. And you were such an idiot, you fell for it. I'd love to have been there when you licked it. You thought you were writing to some sick kid who loved your books, but in fact it was me."

Henry began to laugh.

He was still laughing when his bedroom lights flashed on and half a dozen policemen rushed in and dragged him out of bed. "Thank you very much, Mr Shan," one of the policemen said.

"It was my pleasure," Darren Shan replied.

It was only then that Henry saw what should have been obvious all along. He had been tricked. Darren Shan was very much alive. Somebody had given him some clever make-up, turning his skin white. There was red dye in his mouth and he was wearing contact lenses. The smoke and the sewage smell were being pumped into the room by a machine just outside the door. And Shan was holding a tape recorder. There was a microphone attached to his shroud. Everything that Henry had said had been recorded and would be used against him when he went on trial.

"No!" Henry howled as he was bundled out of the room and down the stairs. It wasn't fair! His plan had been perfect. What could possibly have gone wrong?

They answered that question when they interviewed him at Paddington Green police station. He was interviewed by two grim-faced detectives. The man in charge was called Jack Grest. He was a big man, stuffed into an ill-fitting suit. "You might like to know," he muttered, "that my son is a big fan of Darren Shan. He's got all his books. I don't know how I'd have been able to break it to the little lad if you'd murdered his hero."

"I don't understand," Henry stammered. He was crying again, still unable to accept what had happened. "How did you find me? What went wrong?"

"I'll answer that, you swine," the other detective said. "Mr Shan had an assistant to help him with his fan mail. Her name was Fenella Jones and she was the one who licked the envelope you sent."

Fenella Jones. Henry remembered her name from the newspaper report. And now he thought about it, she had been the woman who had written to him from Darren Shan's publisher. She had worked there as an editorial assistant. After that, she must have decided to work full-time for Darren Shan.

"She was the one you murdered," Grest continued.

"But how did you know it was me?"

"We didn't. You covered your tracks well. But the thing is, publishers keep copies of all the crank letters they receive and they had your name on file. You had every reason to want to harm Mr Shan – even though he never copied a word of your ridiculous book. And when we found out you were working in a chemicals warehouse…"

"But you still didn't have any proof!"

"That's right. Which is why we planted the news story and asked Mr Shan to help us with that little charade. We knew you'd confess to everything if he walked into your room in the middle of the night dressed up like that. And it worked! You were a complete idiot to fall for it and now you're going to have plenty of time to think about how stupid you've been."

He had been stupid. Henry realized that, sitting on his own in a maximum-security cell in the middle of the night. He had a bunk, a blanket and a toilet built into the wall. He was still wearing the dressing gown and pyjamas that he had been arrested in, although they had taken away the cords. He had been very, very stupid indeed.

How could he possibly have believed, even for one minute, that Darren Shan was a ghost? Henry was a writer! He knew, better than anyone, that ghosts didn't exist. They were made up by people like him, simply to scare the people who read the books. Horror stories were nothing more than that ... stories! He had been caught by surprise and had allowed his own imagination to get the better of him. An Irish writer made-up with white paint had outwitted him. He should never have allowed it to happen.

There were no such things as ghosts. Or vampires. Cirque du Freak, indeed! Cirque du Complete Nonsense.

It was very cold in the cell.

In fact, it seemed to have got colder and colder in the last few minutes. Henry looked at the door and saw, to his astonishment, that a thin white mist was seeping in underneath it, spreading across the floor. And that horrible smell was back. Rotting meat and damp, graveyard soil. It must be one of the policemen! They had turned on their wretched machine again to frighten him.

"Go away!" he shouted.

His breath frosted around his mouth.

And then something formed in front of him. It didn't walk in as Darren Shan had done. It seemed to piece itself out of the half-light, the molecules rushing together in the middle of the room. The figure solidified. It was a woman, hideous beyond belief, her face distorted by pain, her eyes bulging out of their sockets, her mouth twisted in a death's head

smile. She was short and muscular and her hands, stretching out in front of her, seemed too big for her arms.

This wasn't a trick. This was real. Henry knew. "Who are you?" he whimpered.

The woman reached out for him. Her fingers clamped down on his shoulders, holding him in place. "Who do you think I am?" she replied, and he smelled the poison on her breath. "I'm Fenella Jones."

Her teeth closed in on his throat.

Wayne Howard, the compère of the show, had arrived...

BET YOUR LIFE

IT WAS THE LAST NIGHT, the grand finale of the quiz show that for three months had, in the words of the *TV Times*, "gripped the hearts, the minds ... and the throats of the nation". Twenty-six million people had watched the semi-final. Even the funeral of Princess Diana had attracted fewer spectators.

"There has never been a programme like *Bet Your Life*," the *TV Times* had continued. "Forget X *Factor*. Forget *Big Brother*. This is reality TV taken to new limits, smashing through the barriers, thrilling audiences in a way that they have never been thrilled before."

It was filmed at Pinewood Studios near Iver, north west of London, and security guards had taken up their positions twenty-four hours before, hundreds of them armed with sunglasses, walkie-talkies and canisters of pepper spray to keep back any unruly fans. The programme would be seen in thirty-seven countries. But the studio was only big enough to hold a live audience of four hundred people, and competition for tickets had been intense. One ticket had changed hands on eBay for ten thousand pounds. A multi-millionaire in Orpington had offered double that sum in an advertisement he had placed in the national press.

As the sun began to set and seven o'clock approached, helicopters buzzed over the studios, huge spotlights were wheeled into place, the world's press corps made final checks in their mobile broadcasting units, and two thousand people gathered around the giant plasma screen that had been erected outside to allow them to watch the show live.

Inside the studio, in his make-up room, Danny Webster was feeling surprisingly calm. At sixteen, he was the youngest ever contestant but, even so, one or two of the bookies had made him favourite to win. He was sitting in front of a mirror, looking at his own face, as a make-up girl dusted his forehead with powder to stop the sweat showing in the hot lights.

With his long brown hair, blue eyes and still very boyish face, Danny was unusually good-looking and all the newspapers agreed that, if he won, he would certainly have a career in TV, either as an actor or as a presenter. But

that, of course, was only the secondary prize.

Danny tried not to think of the black attaché case containing ten million pounds worth of diamonds that would be presented to the winner in less than two hours' time, by far the biggest prize in television history.

Danny had always been good at general knowledge. In fact it was rather more than that. From the earliest age he had demonstrated a photographic memory. He had been able to speak fluently before he was two. He had won a scholarship to a private school and had sailed through all his exams. Although he had never been strong at creative thinking or writing, subjects that essentially required a grasp of facts – biology, physics, geography, maths – had come easily to him and he had gained effortless As throughout.

It had been his father's idea to enter him into *Bet Your Life* when, for the first time, the entry age had been lowered to sixteen. Gary Webster had been a postman until a back injury put him out of work. Since then, he had lived on benefits, punctuating the day with visits to the pub and the betting shop. His wife, Nora, worked as an office cleaner but this only brought in a small amount of money. The three of them lived in a cramped, unattractive flat in a high-rise block in Notting Hill Gate. A prize of ten million pounds would completely transform their lives.

Gary had used a mixture of threats and promises to persuade his son to put his name forward. The trouble was that Danny was quite shy and didn't like the idea of seeing his name and photograph splashed across the world's newspapers. And there had, of course, been the fear of losing. But in the end, he had agreed. He was a quiet, rather friendless boy. Perhaps his astonishing brain-power, his instant recall, had put other kids off. He didn't like his school very much and, like his parents, dreamed of a new life. His father spoke of a house on the Isle of Wight. The money would make that possible ... and more. For his part, Danny wanted to go to Cambridge (*Britain's second oldest university, founded in 1209*). He dreamed of becoming a librarian, perhaps in the British Library (*designer: Sir Colin St John Wilson*) itself. He would read – and remember – a million books. And maybe one day he would compile an encyclopædia, a compendium of everything he had learned.

How many people stood between him and his ambition?

To begin with, there had been over thirty of them. Now just four remained. There was a copy of the *TV Times* lying in front of the mirror and Danny flicked it open. "Know your enemy", as the ancient Chinese warrior Sun Tzu, had written in his great book, *The Art of War* (*Sixth century BC*). And there they were. Each one of them had two full pages with a colour picture on one side and background details on the other.

RICHARD VERDI (44)

He was the man Danny most feared. Round-headed and bald apart from a narrow strip of black hair around his ears, always wearing black-rimmed spectacles, he was a professor of history at Edinburgh University. He was very serious, completely focused. Nothing ever rattled him. Most of the bookies had made him the favourite to win.

RAIFE PLANT (30)

The newspapers loved Raife. He was a thin, curly-haired man with a roguish, handsome face despite his broken nose and crooked teeth. Raife had been sentenced to twelve years in jail for armed robbery. The trouble for Danny was that he had spent that time taking an Open University degree and reading hundreds of books. He was a huge fount of knowledge and – with his unconventional background – he was definitely the housewives' choice.

MARY ROBINSON (49)

The oldest contestant, and the only female, was a computer programmer from Woking. Her photograph showed a slim, unsmiling woman with dark hair swept back and very simple gold earrings. Nobody was quite sure how Mary had amassed her astonishing general knowledge. She gave away very little about herself – although she had let it be known that if she won, she wanted to become a man.

BEN OSMOND (27)

Ben was the only contestant Danny actually liked. They had met during the audition process and had struck up a sort of friendship. Ben's grandparents had come from the West Indies and from them he had inherited a sunny, easygoing manner, treating the quiz – like the rest of life – as a bit of a joke. He had written poetry, climbed mountains, studied in a Tibetan monastery and campaigned for animal rights. Now he was doing this. He seemed to be enjoying it.

Just four faces left. Five, including his. Danny thought about all the contestants he had met along the way. There had been Gerald, the fat, jolly headmaster from Brighton. Abdul, the taxi-driver who had been so certain he would win. Clive in his wheelchair, hoping to claw something back in a life that had been wrecked by a car accident. Susan, who had complained when she had been asked to share a make-up room. So many different people. But they had all gone now.

And in a couple of hours, there would only be one left.

There was a knock at the door and the soundman came in with the little microphone that he would clip to the collar of Danny's shirt. Danny had chosen jeans and a simple, open-necked shirt for the final, although he had been told that the other contestants had been offered thousands of pounds to wear – and promote – designer labels. He had briefly considered doing this himself, but he felt comfortable in his own clothes and that was important. Staying relaxed was half the battle.

"How are you feeling?" The soundman was cheerful as he slid the microphone into place. Theoretically, the technicians weren't meant to talk to the contestants, but Ed didn't seem to care about the rules.

"I'm OK."

"Good luck. I'll be rooting for you."

The make-up girl left with the soundman, and for the next twenty minutes Danny was on his own. He knew he was nervous. He could feel his heart beating. It was hard to swallow. There was a tingling feeling in the palms of his hands. He forced himself to empty his mind and stay calm. A certain amount of nervousness was perfectly understandable. He just had to control it, that was all. He couldn't let it knock him off course.

At last the floor manager arrived. She was a big, smiling woman in her twenties, always carrying a clipboard and with a large microphone curving round her neck. "We're ready for you!" she said cheerfully.

Danny stood up.

He hadn't let his parents wait with him. They were even more nervous than he was and he hadn't wanted to be distracted. He knew that he wouldn't see the other contestants as he made his way to the set. The studio had been specially designed that way. Just for a moment he felt very alone, following the woman down a tatty, cream-painted corridor with neon lights flickering overhead. It was more like a hospital than a television studio, he thought. Perhaps that was deliberate too.

But then they turned a corner and went through a set of double doors. On the other side, everything was dark; Danny could just make out the great bulk of a wall, made of wood, hammered together almost haphazardly. There were cables trailing everywhere, fastened to the floor with lengths of duct tape. He knew he was looking at the back of the set. Through the cracks, he could make out the studio lights.

The floor manager rested a hand on his arm. "Ten seconds," she said.

The familiar music began. Danny had heard it a hundred times, playing at the start of the show. Although, of course, it had never come up as a question, he knew that it was an adaptation of a piece by Wagner (*the German composer born in Leipzig on 22 May 1813, died 1883*). The music stopped. There was a round of applause. Danny felt a hand tap him on the shoulder and he moved forward, into the light.

And there was the set of *Bet Your Life*, with five metal lecterns arranged in a semicircle around a central control panel – looking like something out of a spaceship – where the question master would take his place. The lecterns could have been designed for a politician or a lecturer to stand behind when giving a speech. Each one stood on a low, square platform and came up to the contestant's waist, with a television monitor built into the surface. Every question was written out as well as spoken, and the screens would also be used if there was a picture round. The lecterns were black, and polished so that they reflected the studio audience sitting in long rows, facing them. They looked somehow dangerous – but of course that was the whole idea.

On one side of the stage, there was a giant television screen. On the other, a strangely old-fashioned clock-face would count down from fifteen to zero. Inside the zero was a cartoon of a human skull.

Danny had already been told which platform was his. The numbers had been drawn completely at random so that nobody would have a psychological advantage. Raife Plant was number one. Richard Verdi was two. Mary Robinson was three. Ben Osmond was four. Danny was on the edge at number five. He was glad to have Ben next to him. He had studied recordings of the other contestants, trying to work out as much as he could about them, the way they played the game. The professor and the computer programmer had been the most worrying. He had been struck by how grim and professional they were. And Raife Plant, with his easy smile, seemed somehow untrustworthy. He would feel less intimidated next to Ben, who was, after all, the closest in age to himself.

All five of them were appearing at the same time, walking in through separate entrances, dazzled by the studio lights which formed a barrier between them and the audience. Danny could just make out the security guards in their silver *BYL* anoraks. There were half a dozen of them, huge men, standing with their backs to the stage, their arms crossed, their job being to make sure that nobody came close. The Wagner was playing, pounding out of a bank of speakers. Danny could sense the tension in the air. He could smell it. The heat of the lights was unforgiving, sucking out all the emotions of the crowd and keeping them trapped in the closed, windowless place.

He reached his platform and climbed onto it. At once, one of the floor managers – a young man in a black T-shirt – came forward and shackled his ankles into place. Now he couldn't move. He would be forced to stand in front of the lectern until the game, or his part in it, was over. In the beginning, this had worried him. Now he was used to it. He moved one foot and felt the steel chain jangle against his shin. The other four contestants had been locked in place, just like him. He didn't look at them. He didn't want to meet their eyes.

The music changed. A circular trapdoor had slid open in the middle of the stage and clouds of white ice were pouring out. As the

audience increased their applause, many of them whistling and cheering, a figure rose up from below, carried by a hydraulic lift. He was dressed, as always, in a black suit with a black shirt and a silver tie. His black hair was slicked back and his black beard neatly trimmed. Against all this, his skin was unnaturally pale. His teeth, a perfect white, seemed almost electric. Wayne Howard, the compère of the show, had arrived.

"Good evening, ladies and gentlemen," he began when the applause had finally died down. "And welcome to the final episode of the most dramatic, the most exciting quiz show on TV. The five people who stand before you tonight have completed an epic journey but only one of them can walk away with the biggest prize ever offered by any television programme anywhere in the world. And just to remind you what it is, let's take a look. Ten million pounds in diamonds. Bridget … bring them on!"

A blonde-haired woman, dressed only in a silver bikini with thigh-length boots, walked out of the wings carrying a simple, leather attaché case. She stopped next to Wayne and opened it. As one, the audience rose to their feet. The diamonds seemed to catch the light and magnify it a thousand times so it was as if Bridget had opened a portal into another world. There they were. A scattering of stones, each one a different cut and a different size, glittering brilliantly on a cushion of dark velvet.

"These stones can be carried anywhere in the world," Wayne explained. He had said the same many times before. "They can be spent anywhere. And tonight, one person is going to walk out of this studio carrying them. Will it be Mary, who hopes very soon to change her name to Melvyn? Will it be Richard, whose career as a professor could soon be history? Will it be our poet and friend of the animals, Ben? Or how about Raife? We know he's gone straight – but is he going straight to the diamonds? And finally there's Danny, our youngest contestant, just starting in sixth form. Could he be the one? It's time to find out on … *Bet Your Life!*"

More music. Searchlights sweeping back and forth. Wayne Howard took his place behind the central control desk, facing the contestants. The quiz began.

The format was actually very simple. Each round was a series of questions on a specialist subject, randomly generated by a computer and fed to Wayne. Each contestant had fifteen seconds to answer and if they didn't know, they had three lifelines. One of these was a "pass", which meant that their question was passed on to the person standing next to them. The next was a "second chance", which they could play once the question had been asked. It meant that if they guessed incorrectly, they could try again. The last was called "toss of the coin": they would be fed two possible answers and would have to choose between them.

Wayne reached out and pressed a button on the console. The single word SCIENCE came up on a giant screen above the stage. Danny smiled to himself. Science was one of his favourite subjects. It was a promising start.

"And the first question is for Raife," the quizmaster announced. "What chemical with the symbol NaCl is found in the sea and in the kitchen?"

Danny knew the answer to that one. It was sodium chloride – or common salt. Unfortunately, Raife knew it too. But that was hardly surprising. All the questions in the first round were deliberately simple. They would become harder as the evening went on. Sure enough, all five contestants answered their questions on science without any trouble.

The next round – ENTERTAINMENT – passed without much incident but in the one after – POLITICS – there was a moment of drama when Ben had to use his "pass". He had been asked who became President of the USA in 1969, and for some reason he couldn't think. The same question went to Danny, who suddenly found himself sweating as the hand of the clock began its journey. He had just fifteen seconds to find the answer, the time pressure making it all the more difficult. Thinking on his feet, he decided to play his "second chance" lifeline. And it was just as well he did. His first attempt – John F. Kennedy – was wrong but that didn't mean he was eliminated. With four seconds left, he remembered the correct answer. Richard Nixon. His mouth was so dry by then that he had to force himself to spit out the words.

Richard Verdi had a bad round with FOOD AND DRINK, using his own "second chance" to answer the question "What alcohol is used as the basis of a *mojito*?" The answer, which he got right the second time, was white rum. He also had to use a "pass" in the next round, WILD ANIMALS, so that after fifteen minutes (and the first advertising break) he was looking distinctly rattled. Danny noticed that so far the computer programmer hadn't so much as hesitated. She could have been reading the answers straight out of a book.

The first upset came in the next round – FAMOUS FILMS. Raife Plant was asked the question "Who had the title role in the 1931 film of *Frankenstein*?" and – with a trademark wink and a grin – he answered immediately, "Boris Karloff".

There was a long pause. Then Wayne Howard shook his head – and immediately the audience broke into a mixture of gasps and whispers. It was the wrong answer! Danny realized at once what had happened. This was one of the traps that the quiz programme was famous for. It was absolutely true that Boris Karloff had starred in the film as the monster created by a mad inventor. But the film had been named after the inventor, Dr Henry Frankenstein, not after the monster, which actually had no name at all. And the inventor had been played by a much less well-known actor called Colin Clive.

"I'm sorry, Raife," Wayne said. He reached down. Behind him, the audience began a chant, as they always did. "Go, go, go, go, go…" Wayne brought out a sub-machine-gun. It glimmered in the spotlights as he checked that it was loaded. Then he rested it against his shoulder and fired a hundred rounds into the unfortunate contestant.

Danny could only watch in silent horror. Raife, chained to his lectern, seemed to be trying to leave the stage in six directions at once. He was almost torn in half, blood splattering everywhere. The noise of the bullets was horrendous. The stench of gunpowder filled Danny's nostrils and throat.

At last it was over. The audience shouted and clapped its approval. Raife slumped forward, his hands hanging down. Silently, his lectern was lowered out of sight, carrying the corpse with it.

So now there were just four left.

Forcing himself to turn his attention away from the square opening in the stage – Raife Plant's grave – Danny searched for his mother and father in the audience. They had been given VIP places in the front row. Gary Webster was trying to smile, feebly waving a hand at his son. It looked as if his mother had been sick. She was slumped in the seat next to her husband. Her face was pale.

Richard Verdi answered the next question correctly. So did Mary Robinson. When it came to Ben Osmond's turn, he seemed rattled after what had just happened. "What was the name of the character played by Sir Ian McKellen in the three *X-Men* films?" Ben hesitated – and came up with the right answer, Magneto, with only seconds left.

Danny liked films but he was forced to use his precious "pass" when his turn came. "Who produced the original version of *The Italian*

Job?" In the back of his mind he knew – somehow – that the remake had been directed by someone called F. Gary Gray. But the original had been shot in 1969, almost thirty years before Danny was born. The question went to Richard Verdi.

And with a thrill, Danny realized that the history professor also wasn't sure. He could, of course, have passed the question on to Mary Robertson but he had already used his "pass" in the WILD ANIMALS round. Would he use his last lifeline, "toss of the coin"? Danny glanced his way and saw the beads of sweat on the bald man's head.

"I need an answer," Wayne Howard said.

The clock was ticking. Five … four … three … two…

"It was Robert Deeley!" the professor exclaimed at the last second.

There was another pause. Pauses were what everyone feared.

"I'm sorry," Wayne Howard said. "The correct answer is *Michael* Deeley."

"Go, go, go, go, go…" the audience began.

"But that's not…" Verdi began.

He never finished the sentence. Wayne Howard flicked a switch on his console and twenty thousand volts of electricity coursed through the leg irons and also through the man connected to them. In less than five seconds, Richard Verdi was carbonized. Flames burst out of his ears and eyes. There was a terrible smell of burning flesh. Then he crumpled and disappeared behind his lectern. Once again the stage opened and swallowed him up. The audience was cheering. Two women in the back row were holding up a banner that read GIVE HIM THE JUICE, WAYNE. It seemed that their wish had been granted.

There were just three contestants left.

Danny had to force himself not to lose his composure. He had passed on the film question and so, in a way, he was responsible for what had happened. He had used the second of his lifelines and worse still, he then had to play "toss of the coin" in the next round, GREEK MYTHS. The question should have been simple. Who was the first wife of Zeus? But with the heat of the lights, the ticking clock, the growing tension, his brain had failed him. Two names came up on the screen. HERA or METIS. For a second, he was tempted to go with Hera. It had to be her, surely. But then he remembered. She had been Zeus's third wife.

"Metis," he said.

A pause. The audience waited.

"That's the correct answer," Wayne Howard said.

Danny almost fainted with relief. At the same time, he noticed Mary Robinson sneering at him, telling him that she had known the correct answer all along.

And now he had no lifelines left.

Two more rounds – CURRENT EVENTS and THE BEATLES – and not a great deal had changed. Ben had used one pass. So had Mary. Danny was in the weakest position. With the contest almost over, any one of them could still win, although if Danny had been allowed a bet he would probably have put his money on Mary.

And then came a round entitled UNLUCKY DIP. The audience cheered when they saw the two words on the screen. It was well known that these questions would be particularly fiendish, designed to catch the contestants out. And in this round, no lifelines were allowed.

Wayne Howard looked more devilish than ever as he read out the first question. "The Smith family has six sisters and each sister has one brother. Including Mr and Mrs Smith, how many people are there in the family?"

It was Ben Osmond's turn to answer. "There are fourteen people," he said.

Danny's heart sank. He knew exactly how Ben had arrived at the answer. He had added six sisters to six brothers, making twelve.

Then he had added Mr and Mrs Smith, bringing the total to fourteen.

But he was wrong.

In fact, the six sisters only had one brother between them. There were just seven kids and so with the parents, the correct total was nine.

"Bad luck," Wayne muttered.

"Go, go, go, go…"

What had happened? Had Ben let his concentration slip? Had he been tired? Or had he simply wanted the whole thing to be over? Either way, the result was the same and the answer was no sooner out of his mouth than he seemed to realize what he had done. He turned to Danny. "I'm sorry, little man." He shrugged. "It looks like I'm going to have to check out."

"Go, go, go…"

Wayne pressed a button on his console. The correct answer was already flashing on the screen. Ben didn't move. Danny glanced up and saw a glass cylinder sliding down from above. It clicked into place, completely surrounding Ben, and a moment later there was a hiss as a cloud of poisonous gas belched out from the floor. Within seconds, Ben was invisible, lost in an ugly white fog that swirled around him. The audience was ecstatic, many of them on their feet, applauding. Wayne pressed a second button and powerful ventilators sucked the poison out. The cylinder rose. Ben was slumped forward. He could have been asleep, but Danny knew his eyes would never open again. He turned away as the platform disappeared beneath the stage.

Danny was sure he was finished. Ben Osmond might not have exactly been a friend but somehow he had always seemed to be on Danny's side. Mary Robinson, on the other hand, was ice-cold and pitiless. She would never make a mistake. She would stand there and smile when Danny finally stumbled and the ten million pounds would be hers.

When Danny's own question came, he could barely find the strength to work out the answer.

"Divide thirty by half and add ten. What do you get?"

The answer was obvious. Half of thirty was fifteen. Add ten. That made twenty-five. The audience had gone silent. Danny could see the studio clock counting the seconds. Fifteen seconds! Fifteen plus ten equals twenty-five. He opened his mouth to give the answer. No. There had to be a trick. Think again!

Divide thirty by half.

Of course.

You had to think about the exact words. Divide thirty by the fraction – one half – and you got sixty. There were sixty halves in thirty. Add ten to that…

One second left.

"Seventy!" Danny blurted out.

"That is correct," Wayne said, and the audience applauded. Most of them had got it wrong. And Danny was clearly the underdog. During the course of the show, there had been a shift in sympathy. Most people in the studio now wanted the teenager to win.

Wayne turned to Mary Robinson. "How many animals of each species did Moses take into the ark?" he asked.

Mary smiled. Was she over-confident or had the pressure finally got to her? The critics would be arguing about it for weeks to come. "Two," she replied.

Wayne blinked twice.

"Wait a minute!" Mary's face had suddenly changed. For the first time, her eyes were filled with fear. Her mouth had dropped. The little gold earrings trembled. It was an old chestnut and she had fallen for it! "Moses didn't take any animals into the ark," she corrected herself. "It was Noah. The answer is none!"

Wayne sighed. "That's absolutely correct, Mary. But I'm afraid I have to take your first answer. You said "two" when the answer is

"none" and I'm afraid that was wrong.

Before the audience could even begin its usual chant, he took out a handgun and shot her between the eyes.

The single shot was deafening. It seemed impossible that such a small gun could make so much noise. Mary was thrown backwards, disappearing from sight. For a moment, nobody did anything. Then every spotlight in the studio swung round, focusing on Danny.

It wasn't quite over yet.

One question remained.

Wayne produced a golden envelope. Inside it was a question that had been set by the Prime Minister himself. There were no lifelines, no help from the audience, no second chances. At this moment, it was all or nothing. Wayne took out a silver knife and slit open the envelope. "Danny Webster," he said. "You are our last survivor. Answer this and you will be our undisputed champion. We're going to give you an extra five seconds to help you. How are you feeling?"

"Just ask me the question," Danny rasped. The lights were blinding him. He could feel them burning his brain.

"All right. Here it is." Wayne paused. "Can you tell me the name of the biggest library in the world?"

Total silence. It was as if the audience was no longer breathing. The clock had started ticking. In twenty seconds, Danny would be either very rich or very dead.

But he knew the answer! Danny wanted to be a librarian, and he knew that it wasn't the British Library. That was the second biggest, with over fourteen million books. "It's the American Library of Congress," he said.

Another long silence.

"You're absolutely right!" Wayne said.

Everything went crazy. The audience left their seats once again, cheering and shouting. The security men closed ranks, forming a barrier in front of the stage. Fireworks exploded and brightly coloured streamers rained down. Two floor managers ran forward and released Danny from his shackles. For the first time, he realized that he was soaked in perspiration. He found it hard to move. Bridget, the blonde in the bikini, came back with the attaché case.

Wayne strode forward and took Danny's hand, at the same time thumping him on back. "This year's winner, just sixteen years of age, is Danny Webster. Ladies and gentlemen, I give you the youngest multimillionaire in the country!"

More cheering. Somehow Danny's parents had found their way onto the stage. His father was whooping with excitement while his mother smothered him in kisses. "I knew you could do it, son!" Gary exclaimed. "You've made us! We're in the money!"

The next five minutes were totally chaotic for Danny. His head wasn't working. Nothing made sense any more. He reached out as the attaché case was pressed into his hands and felt the diamonds rattling inside. Bridget kissed him. Wayne Howard embraced him. It seemed that everyone wanted to touch him, to congratulate him. His name was flashing on the screen in gold letters. The Wagner was playing again.

The security men had formed a protective tunnel and somehow he was bundled out of the studio and into the cold night air. But even here it wasn't over. There were two thousand people cheering in front of the giant plasma screen which showed his own image, blinking as he was led out. The world's press was waiting for him. More than two hundred cameras were flashing in his face, blinding him, shattering the night sky. Reporters were shouting questions at him in a dozen languages. There was a stretch limo with a uniformed chauffeur holding the door for him, but there was no way he could move forward, not with so many people surrounding him. His father was laughing hysterically. His mother was posing and pirouetting for the cameras. The security men were still trying to clear the way. It was like the end of a war.

And then, out of nowhere, a helicopter appeared. It came down so fast that Danny thought it was going to crash. What was it doing? Were there more reporters trying to break in on the scene? He saw a rope-ladder snaking down.

Then something fell out of the sky. A grenade. Somebody screamed. A second later there was machine-gun fire. Danny saw several of the journalists being mown down. The grenade exploded. Yellow tear gas mushroomed out. Suddenly he couldn't breathe. Tears streamed down his cheeks.

Two men, dressed in black from head to foot, their faces covered by balaclavas, were climbing down the rope-ladder. They weren't newsmen. One of them fired several shots into the crowd, killing the chauffeur and two of the security men. The other ran up to Danny and snatched the case. But Danny wouldn't let it go. He had won the competition. Over the past months, he had answered hundreds of questions. The prize was his!

The masked man pulled out a gun and shot him.

And at that moment he heard a voice, amplified, coming out of a speaker system that must have been concealed somewhere outside the studio and somehow he knew that it was being broadcast all over the world.

"What a fantastic piece of planning by the Macdonald family from Sunderland who must surely be the winners of *Steal a Million*, the reality programme that turns ordinary people into master criminals. It looks like they've snatched the diamonds and now nothing can stop them as they make the perfect getaway…"

Danny didn't hear any more. He saw his mother, staring at him in horror, and glanced down at his chest. Blood was pouring out. Then he was toppling forward. The attaché case was no longer in his hands. There was no pain.

A moment later everything went black and his one last thought was that, in a way, it was all very much like a television being turned off.

DO YOU WANT TO BE ON TV?

Enditall Entertainment, makers of **STEAL A MILLION** and **THE AXE FACTOR**, are looking for contestants for a brand new game soon to be shown on Channel 44.

In **BURIED ALIVE**, ten members of the public will be entombed in secret locations all over the country and their families will have just twenty-four hours to find them before they run out of air. Answer the questions correctly and they'll be given the clues that will lead them to their loved ones. But will they arrive in time?

The prize? An eye-watering one million pound pay-off, for you or your next-of-kin.

Applicants need to be at least eighteen years old and in good physical condition. A sense of humour is essential. Send a full colour photograph and CV, including your religious denomination.

Even with the windows closed, Jason
could smell meat that was being roasted
and smoked at the same time...

YOU HAVE ARRIVED

EVERYONE KNEW WHO ruled at the Kenworth Estate. There
was Harry Faulkner, Haz to his friends, and Jason Steel, barely fifteen but
walking tall like someone ten years older. When a new obscenity appeared,
sprayed over the side of somebody's house ... when an old woman had her
bag snatched at night ... when a car, or the wheels or wing mirrors of a car,
went missing ... when a window got smashed ... it had to be Haz and Jace.
Everybody knew. But nobody liked to say.

The Kenworth Estate had been built in the sixties. It had probably looked fine when it was planned, but once translated to real life it simply hadn't worked. There were three blocks of high-rise flats with views, mainly of one another, and a whole series of individual houses which might have looked attractive from a distance but which soon lost their charm when you tried to negotiate your way along the maze of dark passageways connecting them. Crime Alley and Muggers' Mews … they all had names like that and the names told you everything you needed to know.

Even its location was against it. It was about a mile from Ipswich, just too far away from the nearest school or shopping centre to make walking possible, especially when the east-coast rain was sweeping in across the concrete. But nor was it quite in the countryside. It was surrounded by pylons and warehouses, with just one pub, The King's Arms, and one fish-and-chip shop close by. There was talk of the whole place being done up, the buildings painted and the lawns replanted, but talk was all it seemed to be.

Even so, life on the estate might not have been too bad for many of the residents who were, by and large, a friendly bunch. People tried to help one another out. If one of the older residents got ill, neighbours would pop in for a visit. There were quiz nights at the pub. Now and then someone would organize a litter party, and all the crumpled Coke cans and broken bottles would be carried off only to reappear slowly over the months that followed.

But the one problem that wouldn't go away, even for a minute, was the local gang. It didn't have a name. It wasn't called the Sharks or the Razorboys or anything like that. Nor was it particularly organized. It was just there … half a dozen teenagers, maybe a couple more in their early twenties, prowling the estate, killing time, smoking, making life miserable for everyone else.

A boy called Bob Kirby had been gang leader for as long as anyone could remember. He was also known as Romeo because of the big red heart tattooed on his right shoulder although nobody knew when he'd had it put there or why. Certainly, Bob Kirby had very little love for anyone. He sneered at his father, beat his mother and terrorized anyone who got in his way. Bob had been a weight-lifter, with muscles that wouldn't have looked out of place on a Hollywood star or, for that matter, a long-term convict. Once, in a fight, he had broken the jaw of a man twice his size. Aged just nineteen, he had been given two ASBOs and was well known to the local police who were just waiting for him to make the one mistake that would put him into their care. But Bob had been careful. Either that, or he was just lucky. The Kenworth Estate was his and he ruled it in filthy jeans and his trademark hoodie, a concealed weapon in one pocket, ten Marlboro Lights in another, and a permanent scowl on his pockmarked face.

And then, one day, Bob Kirby disappeared. He had last been seen driving east on the A14 in a stolen car, and rumour had it that he had upped sticks and moved to London. This was strange, as he had no friends or relatives there. Bob had no friends anywhere. Some people whispered that he had been stopped by the police on the way, beaten up and left in a ditch – but this was just wishful thinking. He had gone because he had decided to go. And the only thing that mattered was that, with a bit of luck, he wouldn't come back.

His place, however, had been quickly taken. Harry Faulkner had been Bob's lieutenant, his second-in-command and the first to do whatever Bob wanted. When old Mr Rossiter's house was burgled and his war medals stolen, it was Harry who had put his elbow through the back window. He was pale and unhealthy-looking, with tufts of greasy, fair hair, cut short, and a stye that had taken up permanent residence in the corner of his eye. His teeth were amazingly uneven and he had lost two of them in a fight nine years earlier when he was barely eleven. He had been excluded from school more often than he had been in it and he too had been served with an ASBO. His name appeared frequently on the lists passed between the police and social workers. He lived with his single mother, who drank, and a mongrel dog that limped around the wreck of the garden and cowered when Harry came home.

He had chosen Jason Steel to be his own right-hand man – something that had made Jason enormously proud, particularly as he was only fifteen and, despite his best efforts, still had no police record. As soon as Harry took him under his wing, Jason promptly gave up attending school, something his teachers couldn't understand because, despite appearances, he was actually fairly bright. Those appearances included a shaven head, hostile eyes and nicotine-stained fingers. Jason was scrawny and small for his age, hollowed out by the life he had chosen. He didn't sleep enough, eat enough or look after his personal hygiene in any meaningful way. He was just happy to be with Harry. That was his tragedy. He couldn't see how pathetic that made him.

The two of them spent their days doing very little. They seldom got up before ten or eleven in the morning, ate large, unhealthy breakfasts and were outside The King's Arms by one. Here they would meet up with Den, Frankie, Jo-Jo, PK and Ashley – the other members of the gang. Of course, the barman wasn't supposed to serve them drinks. But Harry Faulkner was old enough to buy alcohol and the rest of them looked it, so why argue? Keep the boys happy and your windows might stay unbroken. That was the philosophy around here.

In the afternoon, the seven of them might go shopping in Ipswich … or shoplifting,

rather, for they seldom paid for anything. Sometimes Harry and Jason would head off alone. They liked going to the cinema. One of them would buy a ticket and let the other in through the fire door. They took drugs, of course. So far they had stayed off the heavy stuff; both of them were afraid – although neither of them would have admitted it. But they smoked grass and passed hours in a semiconscious state. For all seven gang members, this wasn't so very different from their normal state. They had found a way of making the day pass without their noticing. If they were bored, they didn't know it. And if they knew it, they didn't admit it. They were happy being together. What else did they need?

But Harry and Jason were on their own the day they came upon the BMW.

It was parked just round the corner from The King's Arms, sitting in an empty street as if it had simply dropped out of the sky. What was an expensive car like this doing on the Kenworth Estate anyway? It looked brand-new, although its number plate showed that it was actually three years old. A BMW X3, metallic silver with alloy wheels, sports trim leather interior and electric sunroof, parked there looking as if it should be in some swanky showroom.

Incredible.

"Where d'you think that came from?" Harry asked. He had a squeaky voice, the result of all his smoking, and he almost purposefully brutalized every word. "Whe' d'ya fink tha' caym frum…?"

"I dunno, Haz," Jason replied. He was already wondering what Harry would do. Run a key down the paintwork, certainly. And perhaps more.

"How much d'you think it's worth?"

"I got no idea." In fact, Jason guessed its value would be around twenty-thousand pounds. The latest X3 went for about thirty-thousand pounds new. He'd read that in a magazine. But it was always better to keep his mouth shut when he was with Harry. Being too clever with someone like that could be bad for your wellbeing.

"Who'd park something like that round here?" Harry looked across the surrounding wasteland, back towards the pub and across the estate. There was nobody in sight. It was a cold day and drizzling. The winter months were drawing in.

"What you gonna do, Haz?"

Harry hadn't decided yet, but Jason could see all sorts of possibilities travelling across his eyes like prizes in a game show. The DVD player, the cuddly toy, the twenty-grand four-by-four…

"Let's get another drink," Jason went on. It was three o'clock and the pub would be closed by now, but there was something about the BMW that made him want to move on. It shouldn't have been there. It was weird. And there was something else…

"Nah. Wait a minute." Harry was still deep in thought. "That's a nice car," he said. "And it's here. And there's nobody about."

"Who'd leave a car like that out here?" Jason asked, almost exactly echoing what Harry had said a few moments before.

"Let's take a closer look."

"You think it's safe?" Jason wasn't sure why he'd said that.

"You think that little diddy car is going to get up and bite you?" Harry giggled. "It's safe!"

The two of them went up to the X3. It had tinted windows. The bodywork was gleaming. Inside, the brilliantly polished dashboard made Jason think of a sleeping tiger. He wanted to turn the key, to hear the growl of the engine, to feel the power that would come as the dials and gauges lit up.

The key.

It was in the ignition.

Harry had seen it too. "You see that?" he whispered.

"Yeah, Haz."

"They left the key in the car."

"Let's get out of here, Haz."

"What you talking about, Jace? They left the bloody key in the bloody car." Harry took another look around. "And there's no one here."

It was true. The drizzle was bouncing off the tarmac, sweeping across the grim, uneven grass, hanging between the electricity pylons. It was keeping people indoors.

Harry took hold of the door handle and pressed. It was going to be locked. It had to be. But no. He felt it click and the whole thing swung open – just like that.

Even then, Jason thought that it must be a trick, that an alarm would go off and a dozen policemen would appear out of nowhere, pouncing on them and dragging them off to the nearest Young Offenders' Institution. But no policemen came. There was just the soft clunk of the catch disengaging and then they were looking inside a car that they couldn't have afforded if they'd both worked twenty-four hours a day for an entire year.

"Are you thinking what I'm thinking?" Harry whispered.

"You bet," Jason replied, although part of him wondered whether Harry ever thought very much at all.

"Let's do it!"

They were inside the car before they knew it. And then came the wonderful moment when the doors closed and everything outside simply disappeared and the two of them were out of the drizzle, lost in the world of the car, surrounded by luxury and the latest technology. Harry had taken the driving seat, of course. Both of them knew how to drive, but Jason also knew his place. He was the passenger. Harry was the one who would be taking them for this ride.

"Wow!" Harry breathed the single word and giggled.

"Awesome!" Jason agreed.

Harry turned the key and the engine fired instantly.

Jason heard the soft splutter and felt the vibrations. Never in his life had he sat in a car like this. He couldn't stop himself smiling. Just a few hours before he had been lying in his bed with its dirty, wrinkled sheets, wondering how he would spend the rest of the day. And now this! "Let's get out of here, Haz," he said. He wanted to move. He wanted to leave the estate before the car's owner appeared and dragged them out. And there was still that something else, nagging at the corner of his mind. A silver-grey BMW. It had a significance. But what was it?

The car had six gears. Harry whipped it into first and pressed on the accelerator – and at once they surged forward. Nought to sixty in eight seconds. That was what this car could do, and even if Harry didn't quite manage it this time, they were halfway down the road before either of them had quite realized what had happened.

"This is unbelievable!" Jason shouted.

"This is cool!" Harry squealed.

The King's Arms had become a speck in the rear-view mirror. A minute later, the estate had vanished from sight. Harry was clinging onto the steering wheel as if he were afraid of being left behind. To look at him, you would have thought it was the car that was driving him rather than the other way round. Jason drummed his hands against the dashboard. For the moment, sheer excitement had swept away all his doubts.

Second gear, third gear, fourth … the faster they went, the more confident Harry became. They raced down a series of lanes and before they knew it they had come to a T-junction and the A1071 stretched across in front of them, leading either to Sudbury in the east or to Ipswich in the west. Suddenly there was more traffic. A police car whizzed

past across them without slowing down, and the sight of it reminded Jason that this was a serious business. They had just stolen a twenty-thousand-pound car. This would mean more than an ASBO if they were caught. This could mean jail.

"Where to, my man?" Harry asked. He sometimes talked in an American accent when he was really excited. He had picked it up from watching cop shows on TV.

"I don't care," Jason replied. The truth was, he couldn't think of anywhere he wanted to go.

"Norwich?"

"Yeah!"

"Or London…"

"How much petrol we got?" It was the first sensible thing Jason had said. When the car ran out of petrol, they would have to dump it. Neither of them had enough money to fill the tank, and anyway, driving into a garage would be too risky.

"We got a full tank," Harry replied. He sniggered. "Let's have a day at the seaside!"

"The seaside!" Jason crowed. It was his way of agreeing.

Harry slammed his foot down and they shot onto the main road, bringing a blare of protest from a VW that had to swerve to avoid them. They had turned left, heading for Ipswich and the Suffolk coast. Almost at once they were doing seventy miles per hour. Grinning, Harry edged the speed up to eighty. Jason knew that Harry was being stupid. They had already spotted one police car, and speeding would only bring attention to them. But as usual he kept his thoughts to himself.

And anyway, he had something else on his mind. It was the mention of London that had done it. He had remembered what it was about the BMW that had struck a chord. Of course. How could he have forgotten? Bob Kirby. Romeo. The gang leader who had disappeared. He had last been seen heading for

London in a stolen car and – maybe it was just a rumour – but hadn't someone told him that the car was a BMW X3? It was a coincidence. It had to be. But even so, it was a little bit strange.

He turned his attention to the inside of the car. The glove compartment was empty. There was a CD player but no CDs. There was also a slot for an iPod but neither of them had brought one with them.

"Hey – that's cool!" Harry muttered.

The BMW had a satellite navigation system. Of course, that would be standard in a luxury car like this, but this one had risen out of the dashboard like something in a James Bond film, full-colour and with a high-definition screen. What was strange was that it seemed to have activated itself automatically. Neither of the boys had touched anything.

"Put in our destination," Harry commanded.

"I don't know our destination," Jason said.

"Well, think of one."

"How about Aldeburgh?" Jason remembered that it was a town on the Suffolk coast.

"Yeah. Aldeburgh." Harry frowned.

Jason typed in the letters and pressed the button to start the guidance. At once the screen lit up to show an arrow pointing towards a cartoon roundabout, which, according to the numbers floating below, they would reach in a hundred yards.

A moment later, a voice emerged from the speaker system. "At – the – roundabout – take – the – second – exit."

Harry and Jason looked at each other, then burst out laughing. They had heard sat nav plenty of times. But this car's seemed to be equipped with the most extraordinary voice. It was like an old woman, shrill and high-pitched, not just telling them where to go but almost nagging them. The system was surely faulty. It had to be. No BMW-owner would want to drive with a voice like that.

The two of them were so amused that they almost drove straight into the roundabout even though the counter was clearly signalling its approach: thirty yards, twenty yards, ten yards … at the last moment, Harry spun the wheel and they cut in front of an ambulance and veered from one lane to another. Seconds later they had exited and were following the A14 towards Felixstowe, with two miles to go until the next turn-off. By now Jason was wondering if Harry would let him have a go behind the wheel. He had never been in a car as powerful as this. He would have liked to feel his own foot pressing down on the accelerator. But he doubted it would happen. Harry was never very generous about anything and he liked to remind Jason of his place: number two. Jason stretched himself out in the comfortable passenger seat. Harry would probably slash the leather when they dumped the car. He might even decide to set it on fire.

"*Left – turn – ahead.*" The ridiculous old woman's voice cut in again.

"Left turn ahead!" Harry mimicked the sound with a high-pitched falsetto of his own, and laughed.

"You think it's broken, Haz?" Jason asked.

"*Turn – left – onto – the – A – twelve.*" It was almost as if the machine had heard him and wanted to contradict him. And sure enough, there was the signpost. The A12 to Lowestoft, the coastal road that would take them past Woodbridge and Orford and on to Aldeburgh.

Harry made the turn, then fished in his pocket and took out a packet of ten cigarettes. He offered one to Jason and they both lit up, using the BMW's lighter. Although Jason wouldn't have dared admit it, he didn't like smoking. He hated the smell – and it gave him a sore throat. But generally, what Harry did, he did. Soon the inside of the car was filled with grey smoke. Jason turned on the air-conditioning and allowed the electronically chilled air to rush in.

"At – the – next – roundabout – take – the – third – exit."

"Let's turn this off, Haz," Jason said. Without waiting for an answer, he reached forward and pressed the button. The screen went black. They continued in silence.

It took them another forty minutes to reach Aldeburgh, a pretty coastal town with a shingle beach that stretched from one end to the other. Jason had chosen it because he had been here once when he was very young, before he met Bob Kirby or Harry or any of the other gang members. It had been a long time ago, but he still remembered the fishing boats, moored on the beach, the brightly coloured houses, wonderful fish and chips. It was a rich town now, full of Londoners with second homes. Maybe that was why Harry had agreed to come here. Loads of houses, empty from Monday to Friday. They had stolen a car. Why not break in somewhere while they were about it?

They parked the BMW in a car park at the far end of the town, next to an old windmill, then walked back down the main street, Harry tossing the keys in his hand as if he had owned the car all his life. After the excitement of the theft and the buzz of the ride, they were both thirsty – and Aldeburgh had plenty of pubs. They set off to find one.

About halfway down the street, they passed a flower shop. Again, it was something that Jason wouldn't have dreamed of admitting, but he quite liked plants. There had been a time, before he dropped out of school, when he had thought about working in a garden centre or even training to be a landscape gardener. His biology teacher had encouraged him and had fought on his behalf the first time he was excluded. Of course, she had given up on him in the end. Everyone had. But there were times when he felt a certain emptiness, a sense that things could have been different.

Looking at the plants arranged on trestle tables in the street, he felt like that now.

There was an elderly man with white hair and spectacles, presumably the shop owner, packing away for the night. He was delicately loading plants onto a wooden tray and Jason recognized immediately what he had been selling. The plants were a pale green with strange leaves shaped almost like mouths … for that indeed was what they were. Venus fly traps. Jason even remembered their Latin name, *Dionaea muscipula*. In a way, the plants were little miracles. There was nothing else quite like them on the planet. They were carnivorous. The leaves were covered with tiny, sensitive hairs, and when an insect flew in, they would spring shut, forming an air-tight chamber. That would be it for the insect. There was no way out. Over the next five to twelve days, the creature would be dissolved and digested. That was how the plant fed. And even the most brilliant scientists weren't sure exactly how the trap worked.

"What you looking at?" Harry demanded.

"Nothing, Haz," Jason said, blushing slightly. He realized he had almost given himself away.

"Let's find a pub."

They moved on, and as they went, Jason noticed the old man glance at him almost sadly, as if he knew something that Jason didn't. Later on, he would remember that. Meanwhile, Harry had crossed the road and a few minutes later they were both drinking pints of Adnams – the local beer – and the tray of exotic plants was forgotten.

The rain had stopped and they spent two hours in Aldeburgh, drinking until their money had almost run out, then walking the High Street, sneering at the art galleries, playing football with a Coke can, testing the doors of parked cars in case any of them had something inside worth stealing. By six o'clock it was getting dark and suddenly they were on their own. They bought fish and chips and ate them on the sea wall, looking out at the black, choppy water. It didn't taste as good as it had when Jason had come here as a boy.

"Well, this is a waste of time," Harry said at last.

"Let's go home," Jason suggested. It had already occurred to him that stealing a car lost a lot of its point when you didn't have anywhere to go.

"Yeah. We got our very own Beamer!"

"Right."

"We'll get it home and then we can trash it."

"The tyres."

"The seats."

"The paintwork."

"We can drive it into someone's garden and set fire to it!" Harry whooped.

The car was still waiting for them where they had parked it. Harry pressed the remote on the ignition key and sniggered as the lights blinked and the locks sprang open. Once again he got into the driving seat. As Jason had thought, there was going to be no discussion about that. The BMW roared into life at one turn of the key, that lovely, efficient growl of German engineering. And then they were away, knocking over an oil-can as they left the car park and perhaps damaging the bodywork – but what did that matter? It was nothing compared with what they were going to do when they arrived home.

But it was a bit more difficult, getting back again. Night had fallen and a slight mist had rolled in from the sea. Neither of them had much sense of direction and it was years since Jason had found himself in this part of the county.

"Turn the sat nav back on," Harry said.

"Do we need it?" Jason asked. There was something about that old woman's voice that unnerved him, even though he had laughed about it earlier.

"Just do it," Harry snapped. He was focusing on the road ahead, watching the beams as they picked out the rushing tarmac. Jason wondered if he had ever driven in the dark before. He probably hadn't driven much at all. In fact, now that Jason thought about it, it was quite remarkable that Harry had even learned to drive.

Jason turned the sat nav on and entered his own address – the Kenworth Estate, nr Sproughton, Ipswich – then punched the button to begin navigation.

Almost at once, the voice began. "At – the – next – junction – turn – right."

That was strange, because Jason was sure they had come the other way. And there, indeed, was the sign – IPSWICH 22 MILES – pointing to the left. But it was already too late. Harry had wrenched the wheel, doing what the voice had said. This was where the streetlamps of Aldeburgh ran out. As they completed the turn, they plunged into the darkness of a Suffolk night.

Jason thought about arguing, but decided against it. They were both tired. Harry had downed four pints before they'd left the pub. And anyway, the sat nav system would consult lots of information before suggesting a route. Perhaps this was a short cut. Perhaps there was a traffic jam on the A12. They seemed to be following a fairly narrow country lane and that, perhaps, was a good thing. The last thing they needed to see right now was another police car. It made sense to go back on quieter roads.

They drove in silence for seven or eight miles. It really was very dark. The rain clouds had closed in, blocking any sight of the moon or stars, and suddenly there were no buildings around them. Instead, they seemed to be crossing open countryside, with undulating fields and low gorse bushes dotted around like crouching soldiers.

"Take – the –, second – turning – on – the

– *right*." The high-pitched voice broke the silence.

Harry did as he was told.

Another couple of miles, this time through forest. They had to be on a B-road. It was certainly narrower than the road they had just left, with trees jammed together on both sides, forming a tunnel over their heads.

"*In – one – hundred – yards – turn – left.*"

The left turn was even narrower. Now there wouldn't be room for another car to pass them unless they pulled into the side. Not that it looked as if many cars came this way. They had lost sight of any civilisation. The woods were getting thicker and thicker.

"*Fork – left – then – continue – straight – ahead.*"

The fork took them off the road and onto what was little more than a track. Jason could hear dead leaves squelching under the wheels. He wondered whether they were even on tarmac. "You sure this thing is working, Haz?" he asked.

"What thing?"

"You know … the sat nav."

"Why wouldn't it be working, Jace?" Harry snapped. He knew they were lost and that was making him angry.

"We didn't come this way."

"Well, what do you suggest?"

Jason looked out of the window. All he could see was leaves. The track they were on was so narrow that the branches of the trees were scraping the windscreen. The BMW's headlights lit up a tiny world, perhaps five metres ahead of them. Outside the beams of light, there was nothing. "Maybe we should turn round and go back the way we came."

"There's nowhere to turn round."

"*At – the – crossroads – continue – straight – over.*"

And that surely had to be a mistake. A fairly main road – at least, it was definitely covered in tarmac, with dotted white lines down the middle – crossed in front of them, promising perhaps a fast exit from the surrounding forest. Straight ahead of them was a rotting wooden gate hanging crookedly on one hinge. The gate was open and beyond it was a bumpy, muddy path – you couldn't call it a track or a lane – barely wide enough for the BMW to pass along. It was pitted with pot-holes, some of them full of water. A rusty barbed-wire fence, broken in places, followed it on one side.

"Take a right, Haz," Jason said. This time Harry did as he suggested but he had no sooner completed the turn than the voice cut back in. "*If – possible – make – a – U – turn.*"

"You want me to turn it off?" Jason asked.

"Nah." Harry shook his head. "We might as well leave it on. We don't have to do what it says."

"That's right." Jason nodded. They had picked up a little speed, following the better road. "It must go somewhere."

"*If – possible – make – a – U – turn,*" the sat nav tried again. The screen was showing an arrow, bent in the shape of a U. Harry ignored it.

The road led nowhere.

About half a mile further along, Harry had to brake hard and they came to a sudden, sliding halt. A huge branch had somehow splintered and fallen, blocking the way. Leaving the engine ticking over, the two of them got out of the car. It was very cold in the wood, far colder than it had been when they left. There was no breeze, but the air was thick and damp. The mist had followed them in from the coast. They could see it, curling slowly between the trees.

"What now?" Jason asked. It was obvious that the branch was far too heavy to move.

"We keep driving," Harry said. His voice was sounding a little bleak.

"Have we got enough petrol?"

"We got plenty of petrol."

That at least was true. The BMW was still half-full and, if they could only find their way out of the forest, they would have easily enough fuel to get home. Almost reluctantly this time, they climbed back into the car. All the fun had gone out of their adventure. They just wanted to get out of this forest, to find themselves somewhere that they knew.

There was barely enough space to turn round. Spinning the wheel, Harry managed to reverse into the stump of a tree. Jason heard the metalwork crumple and for a few seconds the engine screamed, out of control. Harry swore and changed gear. In a way, Jason was almost glad that the car had been damaged. The BMW had got them into the mess. It deserved all the punishment it could take.

They had barely completed the turn before the sat nav system began again. "*In – one – hundred – yards – turn – right.*"

And that was odd too, because neither of them had noticed a turn-off on that part of the road. But the machine was correct. In a hundred yards they came to an opening between two trees and, beyond it, a track snaking its way through the forest. Harry took it, even though Jason's sense of direction told him they were going completely the wrong way. But which was the right way? They were utterly lost. He wished now that they had followed their instincts outside Aldeburgh, taking the turning marked IPSWICH 22 MILES. By now they should have been safely back on the A12.

"*Take – the – next – turning – on – the – right.*"

Harry seemed to have become enslaved by the ugly old-woman voice of the sat nav. Perhaps he didn't mind doing exactly what a machine told him but Jason was less comfortable. He hated the idea of having to rely, one hundred per cent, on a tangle of wires and software that might have been malfunctioning in the first place. Maybe that was why the

BMW had been dumped at the Kenworth Estate. Nobody in their right mind would have actually wanted to drive there. Maybe the car's owner had got as lost as they were now and had gone off for help, accidentally forgetting the keys. That made sense.

"*At – the – crossroads – continue – straight – over.*"

Jason's heart lurched. He blinked several times, his mouth hanging open and for a moment he really did look like a child and not like an adult at all. It wasn't possible! They were back exactly where they had been ten minutes before. Somehow, the various tracks had brought them back to the broken wooden gate and the track beyond. Jason swore. He could feel tears pricking against his eyes. This was getting nasty. He wanted to go home. "Turn left," he said.

"It's saying straight ahead," Harry countered.

"The machine doesn't know what it's talking about. If we hadn't followed it in the first place, we wouldn't be in this mess."

And then a light blinked on, in the woodland, straight ahead of them. It was about a quarter of a mile away, very tiny, almost concealed by the thick spread of the trees.

"There's something there," Harry said.

"What…?" Jason squinted into the darkness.

"It must be a house or something. We can ask the way."

"*At – the – crossroads – continue – straight – over,*" the sat nav urged them. The voice sounded almost cheerful. Why had it repeated itself, Jason wondered, when they weren't even moving?

But Harry needed no further prompting. He changed gear and the BMW moved forward again, through the gate and onto the track with the barbed wire along one side. As they rolled forward, the trees thinned out a little. Somehow the moon had finally broken through and they saw fields spreading out, what looked like rough farmland but completely surrounded by the forest. Ahead of them, a cluster of buildings sprang up, made of red brick with weeds and ivy climbing up the guttering. They passed an abandoned tractor, a rusting coil – more barbed wire. The light seemed to have vanished and they wondered if they had really seen it. Whatever this place was, it looked abandoned.

They turned a corner and there, once again, was the light, coming from an open barn on the other side of a yard. A tall, uneven chimney had been built behind the barn, stretching high above it. And someone was burning something. Thick black smoke rose into the night and, even with the windows closed, Jason could smell meat that was being roasted and smoked at the same time. They drove through a second gate, this one made of steel and brand-new. There was a vehicle parked to one side, a refrigerated lorry which looked old but in better repair, at least, than the tractor. Jason saw some words painted in red along one side:

AUNT MARIGOLD'S
SMOKED MEAT
AND BLACK PUDDING
100% organic. Made from only the freshest ingredients

Somewhere a dog barked. Behind them, Jason heard a clang as the steel gate closed and, just for a moment, he thought of *Dionaea muscipula*, the Venus fly traps that he had seen in Aldeburgh.

Harry pulled up in front of the barn. He didn't turn the key, but the BMW stalled and they came to a halt. The two boys got out. The night air was very cold. They could feel it running through their hair, stroking the backs of their necks.

This was a pork farm. It had to be. There was an oven burning at the back of the barn, and the floor was covered with straw splattered with blood that had dripped down from the carcasses hanging on hooks from wooden beams. But the carcasses didn't look as if they had come from pigs. They didn't look like any animal Jason had ever seen. He saw a leg, severed just above the knee. What might have been a shoulder. And, on another hook, an arm. It might have been made of plastic, but Jason knew that it wasn't. It had been well smoked in the oven. The arm had a bright red marking on the right shoulder.

A heart – and a name.

Romeo.

Jason felt his blood freeze. There was a rushing in his ears.

A woman appeared, coming out of the barn towards them. She had long, silver hair, a yellow face and grey lips that were partly open, revealing teeth that could have come from the cemetery. She was wearing a dirty green apron that hung all the way to her feet. The apron was smeared with old blood. She lifted a hand to wipe her mouth with her sleeve and Jason saw a jagged knife, also blood-stained. Harry was standing dead still. He had gone white. Jason was surprised to see that he was crying. But Jason was crying too. He knew what this was. He knew where they were.

The woman was not alone. A man – huge and bearded – had appeared behind the car, holding a length of filthy rope, the sort you might use to tie down animals. Jason caught sight of him in the wing mirror. Then the woman reached them.

Her eyes blazed and she smiled at the two boys. Her voice was shrill and high-pitched. "*You – have – arrived,*" she said.

It was there, with him, in the room...

THE COBRA

THE ANCIENT TAXI WITH its scratched paint and dusty windows rattled to a halt and the engine cut out. They had parked in a narrow street, next to a shop selling lanterns, chairs, boxes and chessboards, all of which were hanging off the front wall and spilling onto the pavement.

"Is this it?" Charles Atchley demanded.

"This is it," the driver agreed with a smile.

"But it's not a hotel!" Charles whined.

"It's a riad," his mother explained. "It's not quite the same thing."

The truth was that Charles Atchley had never wanted to go to Marrakech. It might be a holiday abroad, but from what he had heard, the city in Morocco would be hot and sweaty with no beaches, no McDonald's, no amusement parks and nothing much to do at the hotel except sit and read. And as he hated books, what was the point of that? Worse still, the food would be strange, the people would speak little or no English, there would be flies everywhere and he would have to spend hours either walking through ruins or struggling up the Atlas Mountains. All in all, he would much rather have stayed at home.

But as usual, of course, he was going to have no choice. Charles was fifteen years old, the only son of Rupert Atchley, a successful barrister. His mother, Noreen Atchley, produced illustrations for women's magazines. The three of them lived in a house in Wimbledon, South London, and Charles went to a local school where he did just enough work to stay out of trouble but not enough to make any real progress. That was the sort of boy he was. You could never point your finger at him and say that he was actually bad. But he was undoubtedly spoiled and really had no interests outside fast food, computer games and Manchester United. Left to himself, he would have stayed in bed until twelve and then watched television all afternoon, perhaps with a plate of fried chicken and chips balanced on his knees.

It was hardly surprising that he was rather overweight. Again, he wasn't exactly fat. He just looked unhealthy, with ginger hair that he never brushed and a scattering of acne that moved – almost liked clock hands – around his face. He liked to wear tracksuit trousers and baggy T-shirts, and he could even make his school uniform look shabby and out of shape. It must also be said that he was something of a bully. There had been one or two incidents with some of the younger boys at the school, but Charles had been clever enough to avoid taking responsibility and although the teachers had their suspicions, so far they'd never had enough evidence to nail him down.

His mother and father adored him and turned a blind eye to most of his faults. Noreen had once queued all night to make sure he was the first boy in the street with a PlayStation 3, and Rupert was certainly over-generous with the pocket money. Whatever Charles wanted, Charles usually got, even if he did have to stamp his feet a bit to get it.

It was only when it came to holidays, or any decision that affected the whole family, that his parents would insist on having their own way. After all, they would argue, they both worked hard – and they were the ones who were paying. So like it or not (and the answer was definitely not), Charles had been dragged to no fewer than six art galleries in Rome, to a whole selection of dreary chateaux in the Loire, and to far too many shops in New York, and now, it seemed, he would just have to put up with whatever horrors Marrakech had in store.

Even the airport seemed to confirm his worst fears. It consisted of a single, rather old-fashioned building that wouldn't have looked like an airport at all but for the runway outside. And it was hot. The breeze seemed to be blowing out of some enormous hand-drier. It almost burned his skin and Charles was sweating and irritable long before the bags turned up – last, of course – on the single carousel.

His mood did not improve in the taxi on the way to the city. His first impression of Marrakech was of a vast cluster of low, red-brick buildings all jammed together inside an ugly wall. Palm trees sprouted out of the rubble, but they somehow failed to make the place any more appealing. The traffic was terrible and it didn't help that there was no air-conditioning inside the taxi.

It was all the more annoying that both his parents were enchanted by what they saw. "It's so exotic!" his mother exclaimed, peering out of the window. "And listen to that!"

From a high, slender tower – a minaret – the high-pitched voice of an imam was echoing across the city. "*Allahu Akbar, Allahu Akbar … Ash-had an la ilaha illa llah…*"

"What's that racket?" Charles demanded.

His father, sitting in the front seat, twisted round. He had noticed the driver frowning next to him. "It's not a racket, Charlie," he explained. "You should be more respectful. It's the Muslim call to prayer."

"Well, I hope it doesn't go on too long," Charles muttered.

And now the hotel.

The Riad El Fenn was about halfway down the alley. A large wooden door opened into a dark, cool hallway with deep red walls and a chessboard floor. A bowl of white roses had been arranged in a vase on a low, Arab-style table and there were about fifty pairs of slippers – all of them different colours – spread out for guests who preferred not to wear shoes. From the hall, a passageway led to an inner courtyard with doors on all sides and four orange trees forming a tangled square in the middle.

Noreen had been right. The riad was more like a house than a hotel, with half a dozen different courtyards connected by a maze of stairs and corridors. Even after several days, Charles would still have difficulty finding his way round. There wasn't what he would have called a swimming pool here, although every courtyard had its own plunge pool, like something you might imagine in an Arabian palace, just big enough for five or six strokes from end to end. There were flowers everywhere, scenting the air and giving a sense of cool

after the dust and heat of the city. And unlike in a hotel, all the rooms were different. Some were modern. Some were old. All of them had a little surprise of their own.

Charles was sleeping next door to his parents in a turquoise room with a keyhole-shaped door and antique wooden lattice-work all around his bed. His bathroom was huge, with grey stone walls, a little like a cell in a monastery only with a shower at one end and, at the other, a bath almost big enough to swim in. There were more roses on a table and rose petals scattered over the bed. His parents almost fainted with pleasure when they saw it. But the first thing that Charles noticed was – no TV! No plasma screen. No flat screen. Not even a portable. He wondered how he was going to survive.

They had lunch together on the roof. That was another strange thing. The riad didn't seem to have a proper dining room. Everyone ate sitting on low cushions, at tables shielded from the sun by a canopy stretching from one end of the roof to the other. Charles could barely recognize any of the food. There was some sort of bean salad and pieces of lamb cooked in a sauce, but there wasn't anything he actually wanted to eat.

His parents were in raptures.

"This is the most wonderful place!" Noreen exclaimed. "It's so beautiful. And so peaceful! I can't wait to get out my water-colours…"

"The food is sensational," Rupert added, helping himself to a spoonful of couscous which was a local speciality.

"Look at those flowers!" Noreen had a new digital camera and quickly focused it on a terracotta pot on the other side of the roof. She had already taken at least a hundred pictures and they had only been there an hour.

"More wine!" Rupert lifted his glass and a waiter appeared almost at once, carrying a bottle fresh from the ice bucket.

What was even worse than all this was

that, as Charles soon discovered, all the other guests were equally delighted by the Riad El Fenn. They swam in the pools, drank in the courtyards, took steam baths and massages in the warm, scented air of the *hammam* and chatted until midnight, sitting under the stars as if they had known one another all their lives. It didn't help that Charles was the youngest person there. One of the couples had sixteen-year-old twins, but the three of them didn't get on so Charles was largely left on his own.

He spent the next twenty-four hours getting his revenge on the riad in all sorts of mean and spiteful ways. He jumbled up all the slippers and broke the leaves off the plants. He poured a glass of lemonade into one of the plunge pools. He even scribbled his name on a painting hanging in one of the hallways. None of this helped the situation at all. In fact, nobody even mentioned what he'd done which, in a way, made him even more annoyed.

And then, one evening, the Atchleys visited the souk.

This was the covered market that sprawled across the heart of the city, with hundreds of little stalls selling rugs, slippers, glasses, handbags, spices, plates and bowls but nothing – as far as Charles could see – that anyone would actually want to buy. He was tired and footsore by the time they came out, Noreen now wearing a pair of ridiculous earrings which Rupert had bought for her at probably ten times the proper price.

"Aren't they lovely?" she asked, examining herself in a mirror.

"I think they're horrible," Charles replied.

"No need to be like that!" Rupert said. "Come on. Let's go to the main square. With a bit of luck we might see the cobras…"

The main square – it was called the Djemaa el Fna – was beyond the souk, in the old part of town, a huge open area surrounded by hotels and restaurants with long balconies and staircases leading up to crowded rooftops. It was just getting dark and the square was a fantastic sight, with thousands of people milling around and food stalls with flames sparking and charcoal glowing and smoke climbing slowly into the sky. There were entertainers everywhere – magicians and acrobats, jugglers and storytellers – with fifty musicians competing to make themselves heard above the din.

And there were the snake-charmers. There were at least half a dozen of them, each with their own basket, their own pipe, their own separate crowd, the sounds of their music fighting with one another in the open space. The Atchleys had moved towards the one nearest to them, on the very edge of the square, almost lost in the shadows. It was strange how set apart he was from the others, almost as if he didn't want anyone to watch him – or maybe it was the other snake-charmers who didn't want him anywhere near them. Certainly, he had attracted fewer spectators than the rest of them. Only seven or eight people stood watching as the Atchleys approached.

Even so, the solitary snake-charmer looked exactly as a snake-charmer should, sitting cross-legged on a little mat in front of a round wicker basket. He was playing on a pipe, a dark, slender instrument which reminded Charles of the recorder that had once been forced upon him at school, although the sound it made was harder and more sinuous. He played for a moment and then Noreen gasped, her hand fluttering to her throat. A cobra had suddenly appeared, silk-like and deadly, rising out of the basket and swaying just a few inches away from the pipe as the music continued.

The Atchleys pushed their way to the front so that Noreen could take another half a dozen photographs, the flashbulb briefly fighting against the approaching night.

Rupert's mouth was hanging open. He had caught the sun during the afternoon and his neck seemed to be glowing as much as the streetlamps. Charles couldn't help thinking how stupid they both looked. And as for the snake-charmer…

He was a small man, at least sixty, with very dark skin, grey stubble on his cheeks and a hooked nose. He was wearing a long white robe with a waistcoat and loose-fitting cotton trousers. His feet were bare and his toes looked like pieces of old, gnarled wood. Charles only glanced at him briefly. He was much more interested in the snake, which certainly looked vicious enough with its flared hood, its spitting tongue and its tiny, sinister eyes. It really did seem to be hypnotized, totally controlled by the music that wove an invisible pattern around its head.

"It's extraordinary!" Noreen whispered, afraid to raise her voice in case she broke the spell. "It's like something in a fairy tale!"

"That's one of the most venomous snakes in the world," Rupert told her. "It's got enough poison to kill a horse."

"Isn't it dangerous to be this close?" Noreen stepped back a pace, suddenly nervous.

"These people know what they're doing," Rupert replied. "It takes years of practice. But they know exactly the right tune to play. It's a bit like magic. The snake will dance all night if they want it to."

"That's not true, Dad," Charles interrupted in a loud voice. "There's no magic and the snake isn't dancing. It's not dangerous. It's actually half-asleep."

Both Rupert and Noreen turned to look at their son, who was standing with his arms crossed and a smug smile on his face. Some of the people in the crowd had also overheard him and were turning to hear what he had to say.

"I saw a programme about it on TV," he went on. "The snake can't even hear the music. "The only reason it's swaying is because it's following the movement of the pipe. And actually, cobras are very timid. They're not dangerous at all."

"But look at it, darling!" Noreen exclaimed. "It looks as if it's about to attack!"

"Spreading its hood is just a way of defending itself," Charles explained. "It would much rather be back in its basket. And it probably doesn't have any poison in it anyway. The snake-charmer will have made sure it was sucked out before he began."

"Young man, you are quite mistaken!"

Charles looked around to see who had spoken and was surprised to discover that it was the snake-charmer himself. The old man had lowered the pipe from his lips and the cobra immediately disappeared back into the basket. The few spectators who remained drifted away without giving any money. Suddenly the Atchleys were on their own.

"The art of the snake-charmer is an ancient one," the man continued. It was hard to believe that such an old and Arab-looking man could not only speak English but speak it so well. He had a very cultivated accent, which sounded completely unlikely, coming through those yellowed teeth and cracked lips, but he spoke very slowly as if remembering a lesson taught years ago. "My father was a snake-charmer and his father too. I learned the skill when I was six years old. And sometimes I learned from my mistakes…" He held out his arm and as his sleeve fell back the Atchleys saw an ugly, crescent-shaped scar which could have been stamped into his flesh. "The bite would have killed me had my father not had a phial of anti-venom," the old man went on. "Even so, I was ill for months and the mark of the cobra remains with me to this day."

"My son didn't mean to be rude," Rupert muttered.

"Your son displayed his ignorance and did

not care whether he was rude or not," the snake-charmer replied. "He has spoiled my performance and thanks to him I will have no money to take home."

"Let me pay you!" Rupert took out his wallet and produced a fifty-dirham note. He didn't seem to have registered that this was hardly very generous. Fifty dirhams was only worth about four pounds.

"Say sorry to the man, Charlie," Noreen suggested. She was rather hoping that the cobra would rise up and dance again. Her camera was still poised between her fingers.

"I won't say sorry because it's true!" Charles insisted. "I saw it on the Discovery Channel. It's all just a trick."

"You should be careful how you speak to me, child," the snake-charmer muttered and for the first time he looked angry. His eyes had narrowed and he was regarding Charles with the same quiet malice as the cobra itself. "You are a visitor to my country so you should be respectful of its customs. And there are some things that even your television channels do not understand. Magic, for example, has a way of sneaking up on you and biting in ways that you may not expect."

"I don't believe in magic," Charles retorted. But some of the confidence had gone from his voice.

"Let's get back to the riad," Noreen suggested. "She gave the snake-charmer a wobbly smile. "It was a pleasure meeting you," she wavered. "In fact it was charming!"

The three of them turned and walked away, but Charles couldn't resist having the last word – or at least what passed as a word. Neither of his parents was watching. They were already searching for the passage that would lead them back to the riad. Charles dropped slightly behind, then twisted round and raised his middle finger, a universal symbol that he was sure the old man would understand. Sure enough, the snake-charmer

recoiled as if he had been slapped across the face. Then he composed himself and nodded slowly, twice. Once again, his jet-black eyes settled on the boy and, despite the heat of the evening, Charles couldn't avoid a small shiver of cold. But then his father called out to him, "Come on, Charles. It's this way." And a moment later they were out of the main square and making their way back through the souk.

By dinner-time, the whole incident had been forgotten.

The meal was served once again on the roof, and this time there were belly-dancers performing to the wail and beat of a small band of musicians all dressed in brilliant white. The guests loved it and – to Charles's embarrassment – his parents insisted on joining in. His father was a large, well-built man and the sight of him waving his arms in the air while shaking his stomach around was something that Charles felt would damage him for life. In the end he crept away and went to bed.

It was about eleven o'clock when he turned out the light. His parents were still upstairs, probably telling rude jokes by now – which is what they always did when they'd had too much to drink. Charles was fed up. The heat of Marrakech wore him out and he was in dire need of a large plate of French fries. As far as he was concerned, the holiday couldn't end a day too soon. Five minutes later, he was asleep. His last, comforting thought was that at least when he woke up there would only be another three days to go.

But in fact he was woken up suddenly in the middle of the night. The room was not quite dark. Four windows looked out onto the courtyard and the moon was slanting in, washing everything a pale white. He turned his head and saw his watch, propped up against a lamp. Half-past three. What was it that had disturbed him?

The sound came again, sliding underneath

the door or through the window and although Charles didn't understand why, it sent a shiver all the way down his spine. Music. The shimmering wail of a pipe. It was the snake-charmer … it had to be. Charles recognized the sound from the main square. The old man must be somewhere outside the riad – although surely that wasn't possible as he was fairly certain that his room didn't back onto the street. And yet he sounded so close! It was almost as if he were right inside the room.

Something moved.

Charles didn't see it, but he knew it was there. As the hairs stood up, one after another, along the back of his neck, he heard its body, heavy and soft, sliding across the tiled floor. It was heading for the bed – but how had it got into the room? The door wasn't open. The windows were barred. His first thought was that it must be some sort of huge insect that had somehow slipped through a crack in the plasterwork but he knew that wasn't true. The music told him exactly what it was and, sure enough, a moment later it rose up at the foot of the bed – inches from his feet – silhouetted dark green against the moonlight, its little eyes blinking malevolently, its tongue flickering, its hood stretched wide. Charles could imagine the rest of its body curled up beneath it.

The cobra.

It was there, with him, in the room.

For a few seconds it swayed from side to side as if unsure what to do. Then the music stopped. There was a sudden silence. It was the signal the snake had been waiting for. At once, it lunged towards him.

All the beds at the riad had duvets rather than sheets and blankets, and the snake had aimed for the gap between the soft material above and the mattress below. Charles knew at once that it had entered the bed with him and he tried to pull his legs back, tried to roll out of bed and hurl himself onto the floor. But his body wouldn't obey him. It was doing

things it had never done before. His heart was heaving. His eyes were bulging. He seemed to have swallowed his own tongue. Tears were coursing down his face. He screamed for help – but only the tiniest of whispers came out.

Charles was lying on his back with his legs slightly apart. He was wearing pyjama bottoms but no top and he could feel the sweat sliding over his stomach. The music had begun again, so close now that the piper could have been sitting right next to the bed with the pipe beside his ear. Desperately, he looked down. He could just make out the bulge beneath the duvet as the cobra slithered first one way, then the other. It was climbing up between his legs and he realized exactly where it was going to bite him.

Oh God! He could imagine its fangs, perhaps as much as half an inch long. They were like hypodermic needles. He remembered that from Discovery Channel too. When the cobra struck, it would inject him with a venom that would paralyse his nervous system. His muscles would dissolve. He would die slowly, unable to breathe, and when his parents came in the next morning, they would hardly recognize him. He would be a shrivelled mummy, wrapped in pain.

The music stopped again. And in this second silence everything happened. The cobra struck. Charles felt its bite and screamed – and this time his voice came out loud and hopeless. At the same moment, his hands grasped the duvet and he threw it one way even as he threw himself the other, rolling off the bed and crashing onto the cold tiled floor. In the distance he heard voices, raised in alarm. Footsteps echoed across the courtyard.

And then the door flew open, the lights went on and there were Rupert and Noreen, his father in pyjamas, his mother in a nightgown with moisturizer all over her face. "Charlie, darling – what is it?" she squealed.

"The s-s-s…" Charles was lying on the

floor, trembling violently. He was almost hissing like a snake himself but he couldn't get the word out.

"The what? What is it?"

"There's a snake!" The tears flowed more heavily. Charles knew that his parents had come too late. He had already been bitten. The agony would start soon.

"I don't see a snake," Noreen said.

"You've wet the bed," his father observed.

Charles looked down between his legs. Sure enough, there was a large damp patch in his pyjamas, but there was no sign of any bite mark, no cut or tear in the fabric. As he began to recover, he had to admit that he wasn't feeling any pain after all.

Meanwhile, his parents had moved into the room. His mother was picking up the duvet. His father was vaguely searching around the bed. Both of them looked embarrassed. "There's nothing here," Rupert said.

"Come on, darling. Let me help you change out of those pyjamas." Noreen took a fresh pair out of the cupboard and went over to her son. She was talking to him as if he were six years old.

"I heard music," Charles insisted. "It was the man from the square. He was outside the room."

"I didn't hear anything," Rupert muttered.

Noreen nodded. "You know what a light sleeper your father is," she said. "If there had been someone playing music, he'd have heard it." She sighed. "You must have had a bad dream," she went on.

"He was outside!" Charles insisted. "I heard him. And there was a snake. I saw it!"

"I'm going back to bed," Rupert growled. He turned and walked out of the room, leaving Charles alone with his mother.

By now Charles was beginning to accept that his parents must be right. The music had stopped. There was no sign of any snake. He hadn't, after all, been bitten. Now *his* face

was bright red with embarrassment. He just wanted the night to be over so that he could forget all about it.

"Do you want me to run a bath?" his mother asked.

"No. I'll do it," Charles replied sulkily.

"Well, I'll stay until you're tucked up again." Noreen had already taken off the bottom sheet. She was examining the mattress in dismay. "We'll have to turn this over," she said. "Maybe I'd better call room service."

"Just leave me alone."

"Are you sure, dear?"

"Go away!"

She did. Charles went into the bathroom, showered and changed into clean pyjamas. Then he went back to bed, lying down on the very edge and covering himself with a spare blanket he had found in a cupboard. He still wasn't sure what had happened. A dream? It had been too real. He was old enough to know the difference between being awake and being asleep. And yet…

Somehow he nodded off once again. And the next time he opened his eyes, he was relieved to see daylight on the other side of the windows. Another day had begun.

He was a little sheepish when he joined his parents for breakfast on the roof but for once they seemed to be behaving sensibly, for neither of them mentioned the events of the night before. Like everything at the Riad El Fenn, breakfast was an elaborate affair, with croissants and coffee, pancakes dipped in honey, yoghurt and fruit and delicious omelettes for those who still had room. There were at least a dozen guests still at the table; Charles ignored them all as he plumped himself down on a cushion between Noreen and Rupert.

"We thought we'd visit the El Badi Palace," his father said. He already had his guidebook open at the right place.

"And there's a wonderful garden…" his mother added.

"I'm not staying here one minute longer," Charles replied. "I want to go home."

He had made the decision as he got dressed. All he wanted was to get out of Marrakech. And his parents couldn't keep him here. He would scream if he had to. He would run away, grab a taxi and force them to put him on a plane. He should never have come here in the first place, and from now on he wasn't going to let anyone tell him what to do. If they wanted to go on holiday in the future, they could go without him. Otherwise it would be Disneyland and no argument! He had made up his mind.

"Well, I don't know…" his father began.

Outside on the street, a pipe began to play.

It was the same music that they had heard in the main square – and this time there could be no doubt in Charles's mind that it really existed. The other guests heard it too and began to smile. Somehow the sound captured everything that was ancient and mysterious about a city that had been there for over a thousand years.

Charles jerked upright in his seat.

"Charlie…?" his mother quavered.

He was sweating. His eyes were distant and unfocused.

"What is it?" his father asked.

Charles got to his feet. He didn't want to but he couldn't stop himself. The music continued, louder, more insistent. "No…" He whispered the word and nobody heard it except him. His teeth were locked together. The other guests were watching. The music played.

And slowly, helplessly, Charles Atchley began to dance.

The door was blown off its hinges and there was
Robo-Nanny with a Burglar Blaster automatic handgun
in one hand and a dozen of his school books in the other...

ROBO-NANNY

LATER ON, THEY WOULD BLAME EACH OTHER. It didn't matter which one of them you asked. They would both say that it had never been *their* idea to buy Robo-Nanny.

But it had seemed sensible enough at the time. After all, they were busy people – Sanjiv Mahal, international director of the world's second largest internet bank, and his wife, Nicole, designer and photographer, in constant demand both on earth and on the moon. Their days were crammed full of clients, meetings and reports. They were invited to dinner parties five times a week. They spent their entire lives travelling thousands of miles for meetings in Beijing, New Tokyo, Moscow and Antarctica and seldom seemed to be on the same continent – or even planet – at the same time.

The Mahals had been married for fifteen years and had two children: Sebastian, aged eleven and Cameron who was nine. And that was the problem. Everyone agreed that the boys were delightful – good-looking, intelligent and, for the most part, well behaved. But like all boys they were noisy and demanded attention, whether it was Sebastian kicking a football around the house and playing his nano-guitar at full volume or Cameron drawing all over his bedroom wall or singing opera with a hologram of the complete London Symphony Orchestra while he was in the bath. Although there were two years between them, they could have been twins. Both were rather thin and small for their ages with brown hair that they never brushed, wide smiles and very dark eyes. Put them in the same football strip (they both supported Chelski) and it would be hard to tell them apart.

The family lived in Kensington Fortress, one of the most exclusive areas of London and one with no drugs or knife crime … if only because it was surrounded by its own force field and nobody could get in or out without showing their ID cards to the local private police force. The Mahals had recently moved into a new home, which Nicole had designed herself. She had always wanted to live somewhere old-fashioned, with a sense of history, so she had modelled it on a twenty-first-century mews house with shutters, window-boxes and a proper staircase connecting the three floors. Of course, the red bricks and grey slate roof tiles concealed every luxury that the twenty-second century had to offer, including solar heating, a miniature hydro-electric generator in the kitchen, holo-TV in all the rooms and everything computer-controlled, right down to the

bath water. Even the staircase moved, at the touch of a button. The house was amazingly large. Anyone who walked in would know at once that the Mahals had to be seriously wealthy. They didn't have a garden – private gardens in London had long since disappeared – but they did have a small patio with a micro-BBQ and a vertical swimming fountain. They were a happy, successful family.

All that was about to change.

Sanjiv Mahal was spending more and more time in China. Nicole Mahal had just accepted a commission to design sixteen holiday-pods in the Sahara desert. The question was, who was going to look after Cam and Seb if both parents happened to be away at the same time? They would be at school every morning for three hours, but this didn't even involve getting out of bed as they both went to Hill House, an exclusive virtual school that they could plug into where they lay. And what would they do after that? There were local teen centres and exercise areas. Both children could dive into one of the thousands of internet streams or turn on their PlayStation 207. But they still needed someone to cook and clean, to make sure they were washed and dressed, to stop them fighting, to look after them if they became sick.

Then one day, over breakfast, they found the answer. It was beamed down to them during a news scan.

"New – from Cyber-Life Industries," the voice announced. In the background, hypno-music was playing quietly to make the product seem even more fantastic. "Our new line of Robo-Nannies is now ready for immediate delivery. The model T-199 is our most advanced yet, with completely lifelike appearance and full range of face and voice types (our deluxe models include Australian, Eastern European and Welsh). The T-199 is programmed to deal with infants and children up to any age, and our new Emotional

Self-Learning Software means that Nanny will quickly adapt to become a treasured part of your family. Kids giving you a hard time? Won't eat their genetically modified greens? Turn up the Severity Control and they'll quickly learn that Nanny knows best! Firm friend or loving companion, the T-199 is the next step forward in modern child care."

"That's the answer!" Sanjiv exclaimed. He was a dark, handsome man, smartly dressed even at the breakfast table, the sort who made his decisions very quickly, although in this instance he would later swear that he was only responding to what his wife had suggested. "I don't know why we didn't think of it before. A Robo-Nanny!" He reached into his pocket and took out his Chinese Express credit card. "I'll call them now."

"I'm not so sure…" Nicole began.

"What's the matter?"

"I just think we ought to talk about it, that's all," Nicole said. "I've always looked after the boys myself. I'm not sure I'm ready to hand them over to some machine that you've seen on a news scan."

"It's Cyber-Life Industries. They've got a terrific reputation."

"I'm sure they have." Nicole was uneasy without quite knowing why. "But it is very expensive," she blurted out. "Look at the price. Two million I¥." The International Yen had been the world currency for half a century. "Are you sure we can afford it?"

"Of course we can," her husband replied. "We've had a good year. I got my promotion. And your new contract in the Sahara will pay at least twice that amount."

"But I was going to take them with me…"

"They'd hate it out there. Too hot and too many Martian wasps. Why did they ever import Martian wasps? The boys will be happier and safer here with their new T-199. I say we go ahead and order."

They discussed it a little more, and perhaps they might not have gone ahead with the purchase if Seb and Cam hadn't chosen that morning to get into a serious fist-fight. Nicole heard the screams and the crash of falling furniture coming from the upstairs bedroom and nodded at her husband. "I suppose it can't hurt to try," she said. "Maybe they'll let us have a three-month trial…"

In fact, the salesman from Cyber-Life offered them more than that. He was a small, bald-headed man with a round face and glasses – in his bright mauve suit, he looked a bit like a wind-up toy himself. He had introduced himself as Mr O'Dowd.

"We offer a full, no-questions-asked refund if you are not one hundred per cent happy with your new purchase," he explained over a cup of soya tea that same evening. "But I can assure you, my dear Mahals, that we have never yet received a single complaint. I thought the T-170 was advanced. The T-199 is in a different league. It's the most reliable and human-looking robot we have yet constructed."

"When can we see it?" Nicole asked.

"You mean, when can you see *her*," the salesman responded, casting a slight frown in Nicole's direction. "We encourage our clients to think of our nannies as real people rather than objects. Apart from anything, it helps the ESLS to kick in faster."

"Emotional Self-Learning Software…" Sanjiv muttered.

"That's right, sir. As a result, your nanny will bond much faster with your children – and they with her. And you can see her right away! I'll just unpack the container…"

There was a large crate hovering on its anti-gravity cushions in one corner of the room. Mr O'Dowd pressed a remote control on the iBand he was wearing around his wrist, and the crate slid silently across the room and opened. Nicole couldn't help feeling that it looked a bit like an old-fashioned coffin even

though it had been a hundred years since anyone was buried. These days bodies were all
recycled.

But her fears were quickly swept aside by
the young woman who now sat up and gently
folded back the sheets of soft fabric in which
she had been wrapped. If Robo-Nanny had
been human, Nicole would have guessed that
she was in her early thirties. She was neither fat nor thin but somewhere pleasantly
in between, with an honest, open face, red-
dish hair and a scattering of freckles. She was
dressed very simply in a V-shirt and jeans, with
her toes – brightly painted – poking through
her sandals.

"Good afternoon, Mr and Mrs Mahal," she
said. It was remarkable that she had already
been data-fed with their name – or perhaps she
had been listening to the conversation while
she was lying in the crate. "It's a great pleasure
to meet you." She spoke with a New Zealand
accent. She had a very friendly voice.

"Hello," Sanjiv said. "And what's your
name?"

"I'm Tamsin," Robo-Nanny said.

"All the T models have names that begin
with T," Mr O'Dowd muttered. "Tracey, Tania,
Tara, Toni, Tina, Terri and so on."

"I'm Nicole. And this is Sanjiv." It was
clear that Nicole had quickly taken to the
new arrival – but how could she have failed
to? Tamsin was delightful. As she climbed
out of the crate and brushed herself down,
she moved like a ballet dancer. She was quite
short but that only made her more child-
friendly. She would be just a few centimetres
taller than Sebastian. She also had the most
wonderful blue eyes. Even though she had
been delivered in a crate, it was already impossible to think of her as a robot. Everything
about her – from her skin colour to her smile
– was totally human. *Perfectly* human, Nicole
thought.

"Do you have an instruction book for her?"

Sanjiv asked – and Nicole thought it was
rather rude, talking in front of Tamsin like
that.

But Tamsin didn't seem to mind. "I don't
need an instruction book," she explained.
"I've already been programmed with all my
instructions and I'm quite able to look after
myself."

"There are just a couple of things you need
to know," Mr O'Dowd added. "Could you
show them your controls, please, Tamsin?"

"With pleasure, sir." Tamsin rolled up her
sleeve to show a small panel on her arm with
a few flashing lights, switches and dials. It
was the only evidence that she was in fact a
machine.

"You can make adjustments here if you
need to," O'Dowd continued. "For example,
Tamsin speaks nine languages." He reached
out and pressed one of the buttons.

"*Je suis ravie de faire votre connaissance,*"
Tamsin said.

He switched back to English. "You can also
adjust her physical strength … useful if you
want her to do any heavy lifting. And you'll
find her Severity Control on her right shoulder. That's a very useful piece of kit."

"I believe it's unique to Cyber-Life," Sanjiv
said.

"Absolutely." O'Dowd needed no excuse
to go on. "There are plenty of nannies on the
market at the moment but ours are the only
ones that come with five different levels of
severity. If your children are delightful and
well-behaved – as I am sure yours are, my dear
Mr and Mrs Mahal – then you only need to set
Tamsin to level one. If they are a little unruly
or disobedient, then you can turn the switch to
level two or three. Tamsin will then make sure
that they do their homework, brush their teeth
or whatever – and she'll be a little less generous
with sweets, stories and other treats."

"What about level five?" Nicole asked.

"I have never yet met a child who needed

level-five severity," Mr O'Dowd said, "and I would frankly recommend that you ignore it. Level-five nannies are used mainly on the outer islands…"

Nicole shuddered. The outer islands had once been oil rigs – at a time when there was still any oil. Now they were used as floating prisons for juvenile delinquents. They were in the North Sea, a mile away from the Independent Kingdom of Scotland.

"What level do you think would be necessary?" Tamsin asked.

From upstairs came the sound of breaking glass as a thought-controlled hover-ball smashed through a bedroom window.

"I'd say level two," Nicole muttered.

"Level two," her husband agreed.

"I'll just make the adjustment…" Tamsin said. She reached further up her sleeve and turned the dial. Nothing about her seemed to change. She smiled at the two parents. "Now," she said, "When can I meet your adorable boys?"

In fact, they waited until Mr O'Dowd had left, taking the crate and a first payment of half a million I¥ with him. As Nicole said, it didn't seem right for the boys to see their new nanny being paid for and delivered in a box.

Tamsin was sitting in a chair when they came into the room but she rose up at once, obviously delighted to see them. "Hello, boys!" she exclaimed. "You must be Sebastian. And you must be Cameron." She had got their names the right way round. It was a good start. "I'm Tamsin, your new Robo-Nanny."

She had told them at once that she was a robot even though it would have been easy to pretend otherwise. The Law of Artificial Intelligence (2125) stated that no machine could pretend to be human when it was presented to its new owner. There had been some upsetting instances of robots pretending to be Mexican in order to get jobs in McDonald's restaurants. The new law had made this a crime

– and the penalty was instant demolition.

At first, the boys were unsure. "Why do we have to have her?" Sebastian asked, turning to Nicole.

Some might have considered this to be a rude question but Tamsin didn't seem offended. "Your parents need someone to help look after you," she explained. "They're going to be away on business a lot and they don't want to leave you on your own."

"Are you really a machine?" Cameron asked.

"I am. But you don't need to think of me that way, dear. I'd like to be your friend."

"What's your name?"

"I'm Tamsin."

"Tamsin? Tamsin?" Cameron played with the name for a moment. "If you're really made of metal, I'm going to call you Tin Sam," he announced.

And that was the name that stuck – even though the most state-of-the-art robots contained almost no metal at all and certainly not a trace of tin. But in the months that followed, Tin Sam proved herself to be worth every one of the two million I¥ she had cost. She was a great cook. She tidied and cleaned the house. She made sure the boys were properly dressed and gently told them off if they forgot to vibro-clean their teeth or made too much noise. She loved playing games – whether it was hover ball (she didn't break any windows) or Space Monopoly.

She took the boys on trips around London. Tin Sam loved ancient buildings. She took them to the Gherkin, which had once been an office block but had been converted into a museum of extinct animals. She pointed out the tigers and the polar bears and seemed to know all about them. She took them walking in the maze of dark tunnels that had once housed an underground transport system, and they went swimming in the crystal-blue water of the Thames. Very soon the three of them became close friends, just as Tin Sam had hoped. She never lost her temper and – it seemed to Sanjiv and Nicole – the boys had never been happier. The whole house felt quiet and relaxed.

Finally the day came when the two parents had to be away at the same time – both of them on business trips. Nicole had further to go. She had completed her work in the Sahara desert and was now travelling to the moon – via the Jump Station in Florida, USA. A whole new colony was being set up in the shadow of the Taurus Mountains, and she was designing the interiors of the SLUMS – or Self-sufficient Life Utility Modules, to give them their full name. Sanjiv was heading back to China. The children would be on their own with Tamsin for a whole week.

It was as the parents were leaving that the accident happened. At least, that was what they decided later, when they were trying to work it out. It was a Tuesday morning and Nicole and Sanjiv were sharing a magno-cab – which would ride the magnetic fields over London to the Heathrow Teleportation Centre. From here, Nicole would be beamed over to America while Sanjiv – his body briefly turned into a billion separate molecules – travelled in the opposite direction to Shanghai. Tamsin had baked a delicious zero-calorie cake to celebrate their departure. And she was there with the boys when they came down to wave goodbye. The two brothers weren't at all worried about being left behind. In fact, they were thinking of the whole thing as quite an adventure.

Sanjiv was carrying a heavy briefcase. Nobody bothered with luggage any more, but he had a number of contracts which, for legal reasons, still had to be printed on old-fashioned paper. What happened really wasn't his fault. As he swung the case into the back of the magno-cab, Tamsin leaned forward to help him and the full weight of the case hit her on the shoulder. For a moment, she stood there as if frozen. Nicole glanced at her in alarm. She saw something flicker, quite literally, in Robo-Nanny's eyes … a tiny short circuit that flared up and then was gone. "Are you all right, Tamsin?" she asked.

The nanny raised a hand to her forehead. "Yes, thank you, Mrs Mahal."

"I'm terribly sorry," Sanjiv muttered. "I didn't mean to hit you."

"It's quite all right, sir. I'm not programmed to feel pain. And I don't think you've done any damage."

"Are you sure?"

"Absolutely."

"Well, that's a relief." Sanjiv glanced at his iBand. "It's time we were on our way," he said.

Mr and Mrs Mahal kissed the two boys goodbye and got into the magno-cab. As they were swept into the air, Nicole looked out of the back window. The last thing she saw was Tamsin – or Tin Sam – standing between Sebastian and Cameron, holding each of their hands. The three of them couldn't have looked happier together. Even so, Nicole was uneasy … without knowing why.

Things went wrong very quickly.

It began that same afternoon. To cheer the boys up after their parents' departure, Tin Sam had agreed to take them to the anti-gravity play centre in what had once been the traffic interchange known as Piccadilly Circus. Seb and Cam had been looking forward to it all week. But when they came down to the hall, Tin Sam was frowning. "Which one of you left the lights on in the bathroom?" she demanded.

Seb looked at Cam. Cam looked at Seb. It could have been either of them – but what did it matter anyway? All the lights in the house were nuclear powered. They could burn for a million years without ever needing a change of bulb.

But obviously Tin Sam thought differently. "You should switch the lights off to save energy," she said. "So we'll stay at home this afternoon."

"But Sam…!" Seb began.

"Are you arguing with me, Sebastian?" There was something in Tin Sam's voice that made both the boys tremble very slightly.

"No…" Cam muttered.

"And are you, by any chance, speaking with your mouth full?"

It was, sadly, true that Cameron was chewing a small piece of Astromint gum, although that hardly counted as having his mouth full.

"What…?" Cam muttered.

"You don't mean what. You mean pardon me."

"I don't understand…" Cameron said.

"Well, you can go straight to your room and try to work it out," Tin Sam said. "I don't want to see either of you until tomorrow." There was something in her voice that persuaded the boys it wouldn't be a good idea to argue. Rather grumpily, they both went up to bed. They just hoped she would be in a better mood in the morning.

But she wasn't. At breakfast the next day, things got even worse.

As usual, Seb and Cam came tumbling into the kitchen in their pyjamas, the unpleasant events of the day before already forgotten. They were expecting Tin Sam to serve her delicious organic, free-range, non-chicken scrambled eggs and Beta-Fix breakfast cereal. But they were in for a surprise.

As they came in, she ran her eyes over them. "You haven't cleaned your teeth!" she accused, a frown of indignation spreading across her face. "My sensors can detect seven different bacteria. You also haven't brushed your hair or washed your hands."

"We can do that later," Sebastian said lazily.

"You'll do it now!"

"Oh come off it, Tin Sam…"

It was as far as he got. Tin Sam was holding a bowl of cereal which she suddenly upturned all over Sebastian's head. Sebastian yelled out as ice-cold milk dripped down the back of his neck.

Cameron laughed. That was a mistake. Picking up the wooden spoon that she had been using to stir the eggs, Tin Sam brought it cracking down, just above his left ear. Cameron howled.

"You really shouldn't laugh at your brother," Robo-Nanny explained. "It isn't kind. It isn't polite. Now, go away and wash and then I'll serve breakfast."

The two boys did as they were told. Tin Sam had never behaved like this before and they were puzzled. At the same time, they had to agree that she had a point. Their mother was always telling them to wash their hands before they sat down to eat. In restaurants and other public places it was actually the law. Maybe, before she had left for her job on the moon, Mrs Mahal had instructed the nanny to enforce the rules a little more strictly.

But their ordeal wasn't over yet. Indeed, it had barely begun.

When they returned to the kitchen, Tin Sam served breakfast, but Sebastian had barely taken one mouthful before her hand slammed into the back of his head, almost knocking him off his seat. "You were eating with your mouth open," she explained.

"But if I don't open my mouth, how can I eat?" Sebastian demanded, not unreasonably.

Whack! Tin Sam hit him again – this time even harder. "Don't argue, Master Sebastian," she said. "You should never argue with grown-ups."

"But you're not a grown-up. You're a robot!"

Sebastian was going to wish he hadn't argued a second time. Without another word,

Tin Sam seized hold of his collar and jerked him out of his chair.

"What are you…?" Sebastian began.

"You can stand here, Master Sebastian! That will teach you to make rude remarks…"

She dragged him across the room and forced him into a corner with his hands behind his back, and that was where she made him stand. All in all that might not have been such a terrible punishment, but seventeen hours later Seb was still there and she still wouldn't let him leave, even though his legs were aching and he was desperate for the toilet.

In the meantime, Cameron had got into trouble too. First, he was told off for not making his bed, even though he'd never had to make it before. And when he did – grudgingly – do as he was told, Robo-Nanny took one look at his handiwork and flew into a rage.

"Sheets?" she shrilled.

They were crumpled.

"Duvet?"

It wasn't straight.

"Pillows?"

Cameron never found out what was wrong with the pillows. Seizing hold of them, Tin Sam tore them in half. A moment later the air was full of simulo-feathers fluttering around her head.

"You are a naughty, lazy, difficult child," she remarked, her normally cheerful face bright with anger.

"But…" Cameron began.

"No lunch. No sweets. No treats. No talking." The eight words came rattling out as if from a speak-your-weight machine rather than the world's most advanced robot – and she meant what she said. Cameron spent the rest of the day hungry and silent. It was only when it grew dark that he found the courage to ask if he could perhaps have a glass of water. It was a mistake. Tin Sam grabbed him, bent him over her knee and gave him six blows with the palm of her hand. It hurt.

A week before she had used the same palm to drive nails into wood.

The two boys went to bed in a state that was close to terror. They didn't understand what they had done wrong – or why everything should have so suddenly changed.

How were they to know that, as he had left the house, their father had accidentally swung his briefcase into Robo-Nanny's Severity Control, moving it immediately from level two to level five? That would have been bad enough, but during the first night, the control had gone into meltdown. Robo-nanny had a safety mechanism to stop her becoming too severe, but unfortunately this had failed. By breakfast-time on the second day, the Severity Control had reached the equivalent of level nine – and it was still rising.

Sebastian and Cameron cleaned their teeth several times, brushed their hair until it looked as if it had been painted on, and came down to breakfast as quietly as they could – but that still wasn't enough for Robo-Nanny.

"Aren't you going to say good morning to me?" she asked.

"Good morning, Tamsin…" the boys chorused. They had decided to use her proper name.

"That's better. Now, sit down!"

The boys sat. They ate what they were given without saying anything, not even remarking on the fact that the toast was a little burned and the Bio-Rice Crispies were perhaps a little soggy. Their behaviour was perfect right up to the last moment when Cameron set down his knife and fork – about half a centimetre apart.

"When you finish your meal, you should put the knife and fork *next* to each other," Robo-Nanny said, and picking up the knife she jammed it into Cameron's shoulder.

Cameron screamed.

"You should cover your mouth when you

scream," Robo-Nanny said, and picking up the fork she plunged that into him too.

"Stop!" Sebastian yelled. As the older brother, he knew he had to protect Cameron, but he wasn't sure what to do.

"Shouting at the breakfast table?" Tamsin demanded. She reached out for the saucepan – which was still hot, having just come off the stove – and swung it in a wide arc, catching Sebastian on the side of his head and throwing him off his feet.

"You wait until Mum and Dad get back…" Cameron wailed. He was crawling across the carpet, trying to get away.

"I didn't hear you ask to leave the table," Robo-Nanny said. She leaned down and picked him up. Cameron suddenly looked smaller than ever. He seemed to weigh nothing in her hands. Holding him by the shoulders, she swung him round her and hurled him at the wall. He crashed into it, plaster and brickwork cascading around him, then slid to the floor next to his brother.

"You're mad!" Sebastian shouted.

"What did you say?"

"You're…" The words died in Sebastian's throat.

Robo-Nanny's eyes seemed to have widened. There was a soft light pulsing behind them. A moment later, she lunged forward and seized him, holding him in a vice-like grip. "How dare you call me that!" she responded. "How dare you be so rude! Well, I'm afraid I'm going to have to teach you a lesson, Master Sebastian. I'm going to wash your mouth out with soap and water." And, dragging him over to the sink, she did exactly that, forcing half a bottle of detergent down the struggling boy's throat and following it with a viciously rotating Pulsa-Brush which she had turned up to maximum speed. Sebastian tried to fight back – but he didn't have a chance. Lying on the floor, Cameron heard the terrible screams and gargling sounds. Then – probably fortunately

– after just a minute or two, his brother slipped into unconsciousness.

Terrified and whimpering, Cameron dragged himself out of the kitchen. Moving as quickly as he could, trying to ignore his injuries, he made it to his room and barricaded the door.

It was just a shame that he had forgotten to take his homework with him: ten seconds later, the door was blown off its hinges and there was Robo-Nanny with a Burglar Blaster automatic handgun in one hand and a dozen of his school books in the other. "What is seventeen times seven?" she demanded.

"I don't know…" Cameron wailed. Maths had never been his best subject.

"Who was the first man on Mars?"

Cameron had forgotten the answer – but even if he'd remembered it, he wouldn't have had time to spit it out. Robo-Nanny fell on him. First she emptied the remaining bullets into him. Then she slammed all twelve of the books down on his skull. Finally, she tore out some of the pages and tried to stuff them into his ears. With the last of his strength, Cameron managed to lash out. His fist caught her on the jaw.

"Well, really!" Robo-Nanny exclaimed – and tore off his arm.

"Stop it!" Sebastian groaned. The older brother had recovered from his encounter with the Pulsa-Brush and had somehow arrived at what was left of the bedroom door. Cameron noticed that he was missing several teeth. "I've micro-texted Mum and Dad. They're coming home."

"You naughty, naughty boy!" Tamsin shrilled, hitting him repeatedly with his brother's arm.

"They'll deal with you!" Cameron whimpered.

"But not before I've dealt with you!" Tamsin replied. She reached into her pocket and took out the laser carving knife which she had brought up from the kitchen. "Now which one of you is going to be the first to be punished…?"

Sanjiv and Nicole Mahal got back that same night.

They knew at once that something was terribly wrong. The house was shrouded in darkness. The central computer had been deactivated and all the alarms and voice activation systems were turned off. Everything was much too quiet. Dreading what they might find, they tiptoed into the hallway. Sanjiv reached out and pressed the manual override on the lights.

Robo-Nanny was sitting, giggling quietly, surrounded by what was left of Sebastian and Cameron. She had cut the boys into about fifty pieces each, and the Mahals knew at once that they would never even able to tell which child was which. There were cogs, wires and bits of circuit board everywhere. One of one boy's plastic hands was lying on the carpet,

the fingers still twitching as the last beats of electricity flowed through it. A glass eyeball lay nearby. One of Sebastian's arms, with its own control panel, was sitting on the hall table. They knew it was Sebastian's because the serial number was still visible.

Fortunately, Cyber-Life agreed to provide Sanjiv and Nicole with two new robo-children, and a week later the family was exactly as it had been when this all started. If anything, the two new boys were even more perfect than the old ones had been. They had been programmed with a slightly lower naughtiness level, so although they were occasionally mischievous and disobedient, nothing in the house ever got broken.

Tamsin herself was taken away and the Mahals didn't ask what had happened to her. The two of them did argue occasionally about whose idea it had been to employ her and they never came to any agreement. But then again, they were human … so what do you expect?

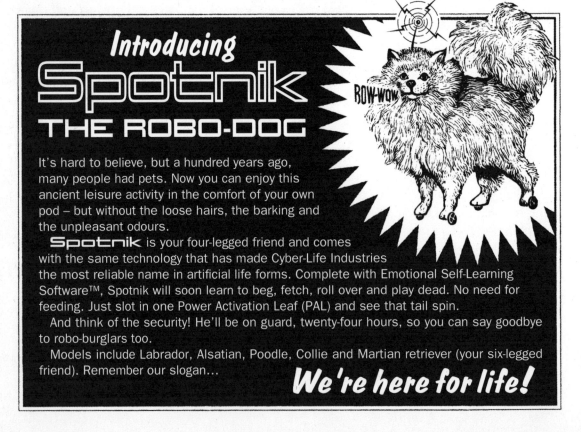

BAD DREAM

When Eric Simpson went to bed
Silk pillows lay beneath his head.
The sheets, a perfect shade of white,
Were freshly laundered every night.
His quilt was utterly deluxe.
No fewer than two hundred ducks
Had met their maker to provide
The feathers that had gone inside.
The mattress was so very soft
It didn't lie so much as waft
Across the springs that held it up
Like froth above a coffee cup.

By now you will be well aware
That Eric was a millionaire –
At least, his father was for he
Had made a pile in property.
When shown a field, he would bawl
"Why! That should be a shopping mall."
An ancient woodland made him frown –
He'd order it to be cut down
And turned into a cul-de-sac
With fifty houses back to back.
In short, he took enormous pride
In wiping out the countryside.

Young Eric really can't be blamed
For being similarly framed.
A herd of cows would make him shriek
And tremble for at least a week
And even flowers had the trick
Of making him feel rather sick.
The city was his habitat.
His father had a penthouse flat
With views of concrete all around
And that was where he would be found
Imagining the day when he
Would also work in property.

We join him now. It's half past ten,
He cleans his teeth (and flosses), then
He goes to bed, turns out the light
And settles down to spend the night
In total peace and comfort which
Attend upon the super-rich.
But even as his eyelids close,
A sudden gust of something blows
Across his room. The curtains leap
But Eric's gone – he's fast asleep
And in that moment he is hurled
As if into another world.

He's running through a moonlit wood
The trees are close. This isn't good.
Why is he here? He stops to think
And at that moment starts to sink.
He's in a bog! He feels it rise
Above his feet, his calves, his thighs,
And soon he finds – what rotten luck –
That he's become completely stuck.
He punches down. The wet mud splotches
All around him, Nature watches.
For it seems this boy from town
Will very soon begin to drown.

Of course he knows it's just a dream –
He wants to wake up, tries to scream,
But not a word escapes his lips
As inch by inch the cold mud grips.
He feels it clinging to his skin
And whimpers as it pulls him in.
He twists and turns. A single jerk
Might pull him free … it doesn't work
Instead the movement's a disaster –
Now he's sinking even faster.
Mud is rising up his chest
He has just minutes more at best.

A living thing, the horrid slime
Continues its relentless climb.
He puts his arms out, tries to float,
The mud has closed around his throat.
He grinds his teeth and tears his hair
As frenziedly he fights for air.
He strains his neck and lifts his chin
To stop the slime from rushing in.
His eyes are bulging, open wide
As if he's been electrified.
Are things as dreadful as they seem?
They can't be. This is just a dream!

"A dream!" he manages to shout,
The words at last erupting out.
At once the swamp climbs ever higher
As if to prove the boy a liar.
It fills his mouth and then his nose
As down and down and down he goes.
It's in his eyes. It's in his ears.
And finally he disappears.
A single hand remains above
The swamp, like a discarded glove.
The fingers twitch one final time,
Then stop and sink beneath the slime.

The next day Eric slept in late.
The maid came in at ten past eight
With breakfast carried on a tray
And found to her intense dismay
The boy flat out upon the bed,
Face down, hands out and stone cold dead.
They told the maid (who'd been sedated)
Eric must have suffocated.
"Surely not!" she cried. "I fear
That something dreadful happened here."
And what had chilled the poor girl's blood?
Quite simply this: the smell of mud.

WHY HORROR HAS NO PLACE IN CHILDREN'S BOOKS

by Professor Wendy Grooling

YES, we want young people to read.
But do we ever ask ourselves *what* we want young people to read?

It is undoubtedly true that the success of the Harry Potter books has led to what many would call a "golden age" of reading. I, myself, am a great admirer of many of the new wave of children's writers and in particular Philip Pullman (a lovely, wise man), Geraldine McCaughrean (so warm and delightful!) and David Almond (a genius … nothing more to be said). And let's spare a thought for dear J.K. Rowling herself. It's all too often forgotten that she has single-handedly taught an entire generation the value of reading, and what is so wonderful is that she has asked for absolutely nothing in return, except for a few billion pounds.

But the question we have to ask ourselves is – are all books of equal value? On the one hand, we have Alice who has such cheerful and blood-free adventures in Wonderland with the white rabbit and the naughty Knave of Hearts. But on the other, there are books like *More Bloody Horowitz* (what a rude title!) which seem to delight in cruelty and bloodshed. And so we have to ask: Are there, perhaps, some authors who are just leaping on the band-wagon, writing books that, far from educating or enlightening, are more likely to harm a vulnerable mind?

As you will have gathered, if you have read this far – and I very much hope you have – I am thinking, in particular, of horror writers.

Now don't get me wrong. I'm no fuddy-duddy. Indeed, in the past, I have been described as a friend of horror or, so to speak, a bloody-buddy. But it seems to me that we are in waters that can become too easily muddy. But if I may put it simply, and in capital letters,

IS HORROR GOOD FOR CHILDREN?

And here is my answer. No, no, no, no, no.

It is well known that children have a much more active imagination than adults. You or I may be scared of, for example, spiders. I am so scared of finding a spider in the bath that I haven't actually had a bath for twenty-seven years. But the point is, we can live with this. Because we are adult, we know how to make the correct judgements. But let us consider the description of a spider in a book. Perhaps a spider crawling out of the eye of a rotting corpse, lingering for a moment on the white, glistening cheek before scampering forward to begin feasting on what remains of the decomposing flesh… That sort of description could do permanent damage to a young mind.

Films like *Beyond the Grave* and *Zombie Stranglers* come with a little number attached to them – 18 – which means that they cannot be seen by anyone under that age. Books, unfortunately, do not have this protection. Indeed, many quite reputable publishers will make their covers as gruesome as possible to attract younger and younger children, driven only by their desire to sell books. I have to say, these people make my blood boil and if I had my way I would sneak into their offices in the middle of the night with twenty gallons of petrol and set the whole building ablaze. But first I would make sure that the publishers, and the writers, were tied to their chairs, unable to move, so they would be able to see the flames approaching, and in their last moments, before they died in hideous agony, perhaps they would begin to regret their irresponsible behaviour.

Of course, publishers would argue, they are only giving children what they want. But do children know what they want? They are, after all, only children. They play computer games and they run around shouting all the time. Really, they don't know anything at all.

So I am shocked, really quite shocked, when I visit well-known bookshops in the high street and see them advertising horror stories in departments that are clearly designed to be for children. What do they think they're doing? Don't they realize there are likely to be children as young as six or seven on the premises, innocently searching for Postman Pat or Fireman Sam? And, while I'm on that subject, I might mention that these books have sold millions of copies without any severed limbs, exploding eyeballs or blood jetting out of severed arteries. As far as I can recall, Postman Pat has never once been savaged by a rabid dog while Fireman Sam has also never been called upon to give mouth-to-mouth resuscitation to a victim with hideous, third-degree burns.

How do our bookshops get away with this? I think I would be perfectly justified in concealing a small meat-axe in my handbag and attacking the shop assistants, perhaps lopping off a few of their fingers or toes. That would teach them to corrupt our young people.

I would certainly like to kill Anthony Horowitz. Yes, I know that would mean no more Alex Rider books (although I'm sure Charlie Higson could be persuaded to write some if he was paid enough money) but it would also mean no more of his repellent horror stories. Now I come to think if it, there are quite a lot of writers I would like to kill. That man who does the Goosebumps series for a start, although they're so badly written that maybe I'd let him get away with a good spanking.

And although there are many who might consider I'm being a bit extreme, maybe it would be a good idea to start murdering children too. I could stand outside the bookshop and if I spot anyone under the age of eighteen buying a book that is not suitable for them, I could follow them home with a huge net and then throw them into a swimming pool filled with poison. In fact, I've got an even better idea. We cannot allow young brains to be corrupted. Much better to saw off the tops of their heads and scoop their brains out with a spoon or alternatively insert a fish-hook up their little noses and pull them out that way – a method used, incidentally, by the ancient Pharaohs.

Kill, kill, kill, kill, kill, kill, kill, kill…

The End.

Professor Wendy Grooling is herself a successful children's author and a world expert on teenage literature. She is also the founder of Read This or Die, a charity that encourages young people to discover new books. This article originally appeared in Straight Talk, Straitjackets, *the house magazine of Fairfields, the East Suffolk Maximum Security Hospital for the Criminally Insane.*

HORRORWORD

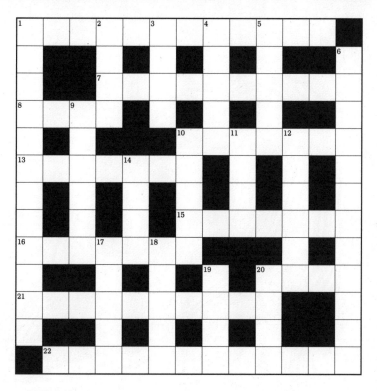

ACROSS

1. Vicious jungle creature. Also, a terrorist once. (5, 7)
7. The man who comes calling when you die! (4, 6)
8. A man-eating monster. (4)
10. A piece of something. It's been separated or cut off. (7)
13. A deadly poison. (7)
15. Kill something with a car. It also means old and broken. (3, 4)
16. Hideous. Horrible. Grim. (7)
20. It's the story of your death. (4)
21. Very, very frightening. (10)
22. A character never seen in horror films. (9, 3)

DOWN

1. It means violent horror. You have lots inside you. (5, 3, 4)
2. Prison for a wild animal. (4)
3. You feel it when you're hurt. (4)
4. You lose yours when you're scared. (5)
5. If this isn't beating, you're dead. (5)
6. A monster made from many body parts. (12)
9. Rasputin, the mad monk, lived here. (6)
10. Fairly frightening. (5)
11. The world's first murderer. (4)
12. Another word for "to bury". (6)
14. A _ _ _ _ of vipers. (4)
17. The bad guy in *Skeleton Key*. (5)
18. Old, dark rooms at the tops of houses. (5)
19. This might be cut off in a medieval battle. (4)
20. To stare at someone in a strange way. (4)

Answers on page 128

With all my strength, I rammed it
into Vladimir Duclarc's chest...

MY BLOODY
FRENCH EXCHANGE

I MIGHT AS WELL SAY IT straight away. The French exchange was my dad's idea. As usual, he was thinking what would be best for me without really wondering whether it would be something I would actually like. As far as I was concerned, the whole thing was unnecessary. Yes, my French wasn't up to much. But my GCSE exams were still a whole year away and I was pretty sure that by then I'd be able to scrape through without spending two weeks being force-fed Camembert and French conversation.

But that's my dad for you. An over-achiever. It isn't enough that he's a farmer with about a million acres of land in the Cotswolds. He has a whole load of businesses too. So one day he's in Wellington boots, the next it's a pin-stripe suit. And he expects everyone in the family to be the same. That's how I ended up with a twin sister who was top in just about every class in school and a cross-country champion too. A mum who was brilliant at everything. Even a dog that probably knew how to read.

And I hadn't done too badly myself. Ticks all the way down my school report. Captain of football. Captain of cricket. School prefect. And in case, by now, you're thinking I must have been a complete jerk, I actually had friends too. We even got into trouble from time to time. I could tell you about the great peeing-out-of-the-window incident, for example. But that's another story. And one that's a lot less horrible than this one.

My bloody French exchange.

I had just finished my second year at St Edward's, a private school not far from Stratford-Upon-Avon. As the teachers kept on telling me, the third year was going to be tough because, of course, it finished with that delightful experience known as my GCSE exams. My end-of-term report was pretty upbeat. Everyone agreed that I was going to have no trouble in maths, history, geography, English and all the rest of it, but it was true that I was a little dodgy when it came to French. This was probably the result of having an extremely dodgy teacher. If you ask me, Mr O'Reilly must have been the only language teacher in the entire private-school system who spoke with a stammer. Not his fault, but it did make learning vocabulary tricky. We all assumed that every word was eighteen letters long.

My dad wasn't taking any chances. The holidays were nine weeks long and before they'd even started, he'd decided I'd devote two weeks of them to a stay in France. On my own.

"You've got to be kidding!" That was what I said when he told me. Or words like that, anyway.

"No, Jack. You'll have a great time. And it'll give you a real head start next term."

"But Dad…!"

"Let's not argue about it, old chap. I did a French exchange when I was your age and it did me a world of good. And you know perfectly well that the holidays are far too long. You usually end up being bored stiff."

This was true. But I didn't see why it would be any better being bored stiff in French. Not that it mattered. As usual, my arguments went nowhere. Or rather, they went to the Côte d'Azur, the south coast of France where some friends of friends knew a family who would love to have an English boy to stay with them for two weeks – after which their own son, Adrien, could perhaps spend two weeks in England? Just what I needed! By the time Adrien was out of my life, almost half the holiday would have gone.

Normally, I liked going abroad. But I felt gloomy as I packed my case, sneaking in a couple of paperbacks and my Nintendo DS so at least I would have something English in the days ahead. The Duclarcs lived just outside Nice. I had seen photographs of them, an ordinary-looking family sitting by the pool, and I had exchanged a couple of emails with Adrien. "I look much forward to meet with you." It seemed his English wasn't a lot better than my French. My dad drove me to the airport. It would be only the second time that I had flown alone; at least this time I wasn't going to be made to wear a "junior traveller" label round my neck.

Nice was only about an hour and a half away, but it felt a lot longer. As I watched the grey ribbon of the English Channel slide behind me, it was almost as if I had fallen off the edge of the world. Nothing was going to be the same on the other side. I had to remind myself that it was only two weeks, that I'd be able to telephone and email every day, that hundreds of other kids did French exchanges and managed to survive. If the worst came to the worst, I'd just sit there and count the days. *Lundi. Mardi. Mercredi.* And whatever it was that came next…

Nathalie Duclarc was waiting for me at the airport with Adrien. She was holding a sign with my name – JACK METCALFE – written in bold letters. Not that she needed it as I was surely the only fifteen-year-old coming out of customs on his own. My first impression was of a small woman with very dark hair, rather pale skin and strange-coloured eyes – somewhere between grey and green. It was easy to tell that Adrien was her son. He was the spitting image of her with the addition of a moustache, or at least the very beginnings of one. He was only fourteen, a few months younger than me, but it's something I've noticed about French kids. They like their facial hair and they try to grow it as early as they can, even if all they can manage is a vague shadow along their upper lip.

"Hello, Jack, I hope you had a good flight," she said, folding the sign away. She spoke French. From now on everything would be in French. But to be fair to her, she spoke slowly and clearly, and with a sense of relief I realized that I could understand.

"I am Adrien. Welcome to my country." Her son nodded at me and smiled, and it occurred to me that he had probably been looking forward to meeting me as little as I had been looking forward to coming. Maybe this was going to be all right.

"Please, come this way. The car is not far."

Wheeling my suitcase behind me, I followed Nathalie to a car park on the other side of the airport and of course we all had a good laugh when I tried to get into the driver's seat. It would take me a day or two before

I remembered that the French drove on the right. It was eight o'clock in the evening and the sun had just set but it was still baking hot, with no breeze in the night air. We drove for about twenty minutes, skirting the city and passing through a desolate industrial zone before finally turning off and climbing up a steep, narrow lane full of ruts and pot-holes, hemmed in on both sides by thick woodland. I was quite surprised. After all, we weren't far from the centre of a major French city. And yet from the moment we left the main road, we could have been miles away, lost in the middle of the countryside. Somehow it felt darker than it had any right to be, though when I looked up, I was amazed to see the sky absolutely crammed with stars.

At last we slowed down and stopped. A solid metal gate blocked the way but Nathalie pressed a remote control and it slid silently open. We swung round and up another steep path. There was just one building ahead of us. It was the house I was going to stay in.

It wasn't at all what I had expected. The Duclarcs' home was a low, white building, very modern with roofs that slanted at strange angles and windows the size of whole walls. These could slide back, opening the inside to the terrace, the garden and the darkly inviting swimming pool. The house stood on the side of a hill, entirely surrounded by trees, with Nice no more than a scattering of bright lights, far below. Madame Duclarc drove straight towards a double garage, built into the hillside under the house. There must have been some sort of sensor. The doors rolled open to let her in.

Inside, the house was even more unusual, with walls of naked concrete, metal staircases and glass-bottomed corridors giving me the impression of a sort of fortress – though, again, a very modern one. The Duclarcs seemed to like neon tubes, so one room would glow red, another green, while the main living area, with its open-plan kitchen, steel fireplace, spiral staircase and huge wooden table, reminded me of a theatre stage.

Adrien's dad was called Patrick (pronounced Pat-reek) and he greeted me in French that was rather more difficult to understand, swallowing his words before they had time to come out of his mouth. But he was still friendly enough; a slim, athletic, curly-haired man – as pale as his wife and son. Adrien was their only child but there was another member of the family at the table, waiting to eat and, I have to say, I didn't like him from the start.

The Duclarc family had once lived in Eastern Europe and this was one of their distant relatives, over on a visit. He was Patrick's uncle or second cousin or something like that … it was explained to me, but I didn't quite manage to follow the French. My first thought was that he was ill. His hair was long and silver, hanging down just past his collar, looking as if it had never been brushed. He wasn't exactly thin, but he had a sort of half-starved look, as if he hadn't eaten for a week. The way he sat, hunched over the table, you could imagine all the interlocking bones, holding him together under his strange, old-fashioned clothes. I've already said it was boiling hot. Even so, this uncle was dressed in black trousers, boots, a white shirt and a loose-fitting black jacket that hung off him almost like a cape.

His name, I was told, was Vladimir Duclarc. I would have guessed he was about fifty years old but I could have been wrong. His grey skin, his gnarled fingers and his hunched shoulders could have suggested someone much older. And yet, he had a certain energy. When he turned and looked at me, I saw something come alive in his eyes. It was there just for an instant, a sort of flame. He nodded at me but didn't speak. In fact he spoke very little. French, I later learned, was his second language.

We sat down to dinner. I was feeling much more cheerful by now. For a start, the food was excellent. Smoked ham, fresh bread, three or four salads, a huge plate of cheese … all the food that the French do so well but which never quite tastes the same when you eat it at home in England. I noticed that Adrien drank wine and although I was offered it, I stuck to Coke. The parents asked me a lot of questions about myself, my home in Burford, my family and all the rest of it. It would have been a nice evening.

Except there was something about Vladimir Duclarc that spoiled it. Every time I looked up, he seemed to be staring at me, as if he knew something I didn't. As if he were weighing me up. He ate very little. In fact he didn't touch the salad, toying instead with a piece or raw ham, which he chewed between small, sharp teeth, and even as he swallowed it with a little red wine, I could tell he would much rather have been eating something else. Me, perhaps. That was the impression he gave.

And one other thing happened during that meal. Nathalie Duclarc had cooked some really delicious hot snacks. I'm not sure what you'd call them. They were slices of bread, dipped in olive oil, with tomato and mozzarella, baked in the oven. My mother made something very similar and, as I helped myself to a second portion, I managed to stretch my French vocabulary enough to say that she also used garlic in her recipe.

There was a sudden silence at the table. I wondered if I'd chosen the wrong word for garlic. But it was l'ail. I was sure of it.

"We never eat garlic in this family," Patrick said.

"Oh?" I wasn't sure what to say.

"My cousin Vladimir dislikes it."

"I hate garlic." Vladimir Duclarc spoke the words as if I had deliberately offended him.

"I'm very sorry…"

Next to me, Adrien was fidgeting. Then

Patrick reached out and poured some more wine and everyone began talking again. The incident was forgotten – although I would remember it again in days to come.

And the next few days were great. Patrick drove Adrien and me over to Monaco and we looked at all the million-pound cars and ten-million pound yachts scattered around. We explored Nice – the markets, the cafés, the beach and so on. I went paragliding for the first time. We went to a couple of museums and an aquarium. I was beginning to think that maybe my dad had been right after all. I could actually feel my French getting better. I still found it hard to actually *say* anything very sensible, but I understood most of what Adrien and Nathalie said to me.

The only problem was that I wasn't sleeping very well. It was hard to say why. It was hot and there was always a lone mosquito whining in my ear. Also, the bedroom was down a flight of stairs, underneath the main bulk of the house, and it never seemed to have enough air. But it was something more than that. I felt uneasy. I was having bad dreams. One night I was sure I heard wolves howling in the woods near the house. I mentioned this to Patrick and he smiled at me. Apparently, there *were* wolves in the area. The locals often heard them. There was absolutely nothing to worry about. But there was still something about them that kept me awake long into the night.

And then there was Vladimir Duclarc.

It must have been the third or fourth day of my visit when I realized something else that was rather strange about him. He never went outside in the day. You'd think that with a huge swimming pool, local markets and the sea, there would be plenty of reasons for him to go outdoors, but in fact I never saw him until after eight o'clock, when the sun set. He spent long periods in his room – and never talked about what he had been doing. Only when

the darkness came would he walk out onto the terrace, craning his long neck and half-closing his eyes as he took in the scented evening air.

One night he went out on his own. I actually saw him walking down the stairs, past the swimming pool and on towards the main gate, his footsteps so light that he seemed to be almost floating in the air. He didn't have a car and as far as I knew he couldn't drive. Nathalie was preparing dinner and there was no sign of Adrien, so – on a whim – I followed him. I wasn't really doing anything. I mean, I was just playing a game, really. But it just seemed so odd for him to be disappearing into the darkness that I couldn't help wondering where he was going and what he would do when he got there.

I reached the gate. There it was in front of me, a solid wall of sheet metal that had been stained by rust or rain. It hadn't opened, but suddenly there was no sign of Monsieur Duclarc. He had vanished. I knew it wasn't possible. He would have had to open the gate electronically to get out onto the main road, even if he was walking. But it hadn't moved. So where was he? I looked first one way, then another. Could he be hiding in the darkness? Was he watching me even now? No. That made no sense and, besides, I was certain he hadn't seen me. Something caught my eye and I glanced upwards. A bat, almost invisible against the night sky, fluttered over my head like a piece of charred paper caught in a gust of wind. It was there and then it was gone.

And so was Vladimir Duclarc.

I didn't have much appetite that night. The empty chair on the opposite side of the table was somehow threatening. I could imagine an invisible man sitting there, his eyes fixed on me. For the first time, I felt homesick. I was even tempted to call my parents and ask them to let me return.

Perhaps I should have mentioned that I actually had a problem with the phones. It turned out that there was no mobile signal at the Duclarc's home and although they would have happily let me use their landline, it was right in the middle of the hallway where everyone would have been able to hear, and anyway I didn't like to ask. I'd brought my laptop with me, though, and I swapped emails every evening. Isabelle, my sister, had written a couple of times (assuring me that she wasn't missing me) and Mum and Dad had given me the latest news ... a new tractor arriving, the wind turbine at the bottom of the garden breaking down, local gossip from the village. It all sounded so normal that once again I couldn't help feeling very far away. Not just another country but another planet.

It was on the sixth day of my visit that it all really went wrong. That was when I saw the mirror without the reflection.

Vladmir Duclarc had a bedroom at the end of the same corridor as mine. The house had a sort of guest annexe, a lower floor that was built onto the side – and that was where the two of us were staying, slightly apart from the rest of the family. Most of the time (and certainly during the day) he kept his door shut. But I had seen inside a couple of times on my way to bed.

The room was as modern as the rest of the house, with an abstract painting – splodges of black and red – on one wall opposite the bed. The walls were grey concrete and the floor some sort of Scandanavian wood. Only the bed was antique, a four-poster that looked particularly uncomfortable and out of keeping with everything else. The room had one interesting feature. There was a full-size mirror on one wall which actually swung open to reveal a walk-in closet behind. This was full of clothes which I assumed must belong to Nathalie and Patrick.

I'd originally been shown the room by Adrien when he had first taken me round the house and I had noticed the mirror as I walked past. Or rather, I'd noticed myself – the fair hair, the freckles and all the rest of it. Well, on the sixth day, as I was on my way to dinner, I glanced down the corridor and saw Vladimir Duclarc, standing next to the bed, fiddling with the cuff of the shirt he was wearing. He didn't notice me – which was just as well because I stopped, wide-eyed, my whole body frozen as if a thousand volts of electricity had just been jammed through me.

Vladimir Duclarc had no reflection.

Now, I know what you're thinking. You're thinking that I'd got the angles wrong and that I simply couldn't see the reflection from where I was standing. But it wasn't like that. He was right in front of the mirror. Inches away from it. And there was no sign of him in the glass. Just vague shapes. He had no reflection!

And then the worst possible thing happened. I must have moved or made a sound, because Vladimir glanced up and saw me staring at him. He was angry. I saw that strange fire in his eyes as his head turned towards me. He knew what I had seen. At once I muttered something that made no sense in French or English and hurried back to my room, closing the door behind me. But it was already too late. Why hadn't I moved away immediately, before he'd spotted me?

I stood there with my heart thumping, every one of my fingers prickling with fear. Perhaps I hadn't worked it out yet. Or perhaps I'd worked it out long before but had been trying to ignore it. All the evidence, spread out in front of me, one piece after another. How could I have been so dumb?

Vladimir Duclarc never went out in the light.

He hated garlic.

He came from Eastern Europe.

He had somehow managed to vanish in front of the main gate, seconds before I had seen a bat flickering away.

And he had no reflection.

And there was one last thing, one final piece of evidence that somehow entered my thoughts right then. Barely breathing, I went into the bathroom. I'd had a shower earlier that evening and the mirror was still steamed up. Slowly, I extended a finger and wrote a word in capital letters.

DUCLARC

Then I began crossing out the letters. It wasn't an anagram, but it was close enough. Take out a C and replace it with an A. Then jumble it around and what did you get?

DRACULA

So here's a question for you. Your starter for ten. Do you believe in vampires? I didn't. Which is to say, I'd read books and I'd seen films and I'd always comforted myself with the thought that they were all made up. But that was then. That was before I found myself hundreds of miles from home in a house full of strangers in the middle of a wood with wolves howling in the night and a man in the next room with no reflection.

Now I remembered that vampires had been around for hundreds of years, that thousands of stories had been written about them. If vampires didn't exist, why had so many writers taken an interest? And there was something else. Dracula, the king of the vampires, had certainly been a real person. We'd once talked about him at school, in history. What was his first name? Oh God! It was Vlad. Vlad the Impaler, born in Transylvania (Eastern Europe) in the fifteenth century. Historical fact!

Even then, standing on my own, I tried to convince myself that I was wrong. There had to be a simple explanation. Lots of people don't like garlic. It could just be a coincidence that Vladimir's surname was so close to Vlad

the Impaler's. I told myself that he didn't even look like a vampire. But then I remembered the long hair, the pale skin, the clothes that were at least fifty years out of date and I knew it wasn't true. If there had been a magazine devoted to vampires, he would have made the front page.

My first instinct was to run, to get away from the house and somehow find my way to a local police station. But I knew that was crazy. The police would never believe me. They'd think I was a stupid fifteen-year-old English boy and they would drive me straight back to the house, and if there was one sure way for me to end up with my throat torn out and my blood drained, that was it. Could I contact my parents? The mobile wouldn't work but there was still my computer. Yes. That was what I would do. I glanced at my watch. It was five past eight. I was already late for dinner. But the family could wait.

I grabbed my laptop and wrenched it open. My hands were trembling so much that I had to jab down three times before I hit the START button. And then the computer seemed to take an hour to boot up. But at last the screen was glowing in front of me. The house had no Wi-Fi but I'd be able to connect over the telephone line. I'd already done so half a dozen times.

But this time it didn't work.

I double-clicked on the AOL icon and managed to get the home page on the screen. There was nothing wrong with the computer. But every time I tried to dial out, I got an engaged tone. I must have tried twenty times before I suddenly heard Nathalie Duclarc's voice, calling me from upstairs.

"Jack? Dinner is ready!"

Once again I froze. The computer bleeped uselessly in front of me. What was I to do? Join the family and try to pretend nothing had happened? Or make a break for it? There was only one answer to that. The gate was locked and, unlike Vladimir Duclarc, I couldn't turn myself into a bat and fly over the top. And even if I did manage to get out into the lane, they'd catch up with me before I reached the main road. Right now it was night. The darkness was my enemy. If I could somehow hold myself together until sunrise, if I could survive, then I could take action. Maybe they'd take me into Nice tomorrow. I could slip away and check in at the airport before they knew I'd gone. All I had to do was to pretend that nothing had happened. Vladimir Duclarc had seen me outside his room. But despite what I had feared earlier, there was always a chance that he believed his secret was safe. I just had to be very, very careful.

I left the room and climbed up the concrete stairs that led to the main living room, feeling I knew exactly how a condemned man must feel on his way to the scaffold. The entire family was already around the table and nobody seemed to take much notice of me as I sat down. I noticed Vladimir Duclarc was eating more hungrily than usual. Dinner that night was steak. My own meat had already been served. It was sitting in the middle of the plate with blood all around it. Patrick said something and passed me the vegetables. I didn't understand his words, in fact they echoed in my ears. I helped myself to a few pieces of broccoli and some potatoes. I had no idea how I would get through the next hour.

Fortunately, nobody seemed to notice that I was freaking out. Or maybe they were just pretending. Vladimir glanced at me a couple of times but said nothing. Nathalie asked me if I was feeling well and I told her that I might have had too much sun.

"You've hardly eaten anything, Jack," she said.

"I'm sorry." I'd barely had two mouthfuls of the steak. "I'm not very hungry."

"You don't like your steak *sanglant*?"

Sanglant. The French for bloody.

"It's fine…" But it wasn't. I've always liked meat but right then I could have become a vegetarian in the blink of an eye. When I sliced off a piece of the steak with my knife, I didn't feel hungry. I felt like a surgeon in an operating theatre.

Patrick poured himself a glass of red wine. As I saw the liquid tumbling out of the bottle I could only imagine something very similar pouring from my own neck. "You must get an early night, Jack," he said. "We need to look after you."

And this is what I was thinking: were they all vampires or was it just cousin Vladimir? True, the others were all very pale. They all had the same, uncomfortable eyes. But surely they were normal? After all, Adrien and his parents had come out with me into the sunlight. Perhaps it was only Vladimir who was the vampire and the rest of them were, as they had told me, distant relatives. They were similar to vampires but they weren't actually vampires themselves. That would make sense. But even if they weren't blood-guzzlers, they still knew about their cousin. Their blood relative. They were protecting him. And that made them as bad as him, however you looked at it.

I had to fight my way to the end of the meal. But at last I was able to stand up and go to bed. There was one last thing I had to know. "Is there a problem with the telephone?" I asked.

Patrick Duclarc glanced sharply in my direction.

"I tried to send an email…" I added. "I just wanted to tell my parents about the market we visited today. My mother loves markets. It was a great market." I realized I was babbling and shut my mouth.

"Yes," Patrick nodded. "The telephone line is broken."

Nathalie smiled at me but her eyes were cold. "The engineers will come tomorrow."

"You can telephone your parents then," Adrien added, although there was no need.

"Right." I forced a smile. "Good night, then."

"Good night, Jack."

They were still watching me as I went back downstairs to my room.

I went to sleep. It took me four hours to drop off and by the time I finally closed my eyes the bed felt like a sack of potatoes that's been left out in the rain, but somehow I managed it. The next thing I knew, incredibly, it was ten o'clock and the sun was streaming in through the window. My clothes were scattered across the floor where I had left them. And there were no punctures on my neck, my wrists or anywhere else.

And here's the funny thing. With the coming of light, I began to doubt myself. My dad had always said that I had an overactive imagination, and I really did wonder if I hadn't allowed my thoughts to run away with themselves the night before. The garlic, the hatred of light, the absent reflection, the name … it was true that they all pointed to only one conclusion. But vampires didn't really exist. Everyone knew that. What would my parents say if I asked them to take me home because I was scared? My sister would never let me live it down.

When I went up for breakfast, Nathalie was in the kitchen and she looked utterly normal, pleased to see me. "Are you feeing better, Jack?" she asked me.

"Yes, thank you."

"Please. Help yourself!"

There were croissants and honey on the table. Coffee and orange juice. I glanced out of the window and saw Adrien, already in the swimming pool. An ordinary family on an ordinary day.

"We thought we would go to Antibes this afternoon," Nathalie went on. "There is the Château Grimaldi which may interest you. Also, there is a very beautiful cathedral, which we can visit."

It was almost as if she had said it on purpose, to prove to me that I had imagined everything the night before. "A cathedral?" I repeated. "Are you coming?"

"But of course. Adrien and I will come with you."

If she and Adrien were vampires, if they had even a drop of vampire blood in them, they wouldn't possibly be able to enter a holy place like a cathedral. That was when I decided that I wouldn't make a break for it after all. It was also when I made my single worst mistake: I decided that I would put Vladimir Duclarc to the test. One small experiment and I would know exactly what he was. And if I was proved right, then I would contact my parents and nobody would be able to argue with me.

I spent the morning swimming and sunbathing with Adrien. We played ping-pong – there was a table in the garage – and chatted as if nothing had happened. Just after lunch we drove down the coast to Antibes, which was an impressive, densely packed town shielded from the water by a huge sea wall. The cathedral was a striking, strangely modern-looking building – all orange, white and yellow – next to the château Nathalie had mentioned, but to be honest I don't remember much about it. Because this was where I was going to put my plan into action. And I had to do it without being seen.

Nathalie and Adrien had both gone into the cathedral ahead of me – and I'd noticed that neither of them had so much as hesitated. I went in third and as I passed through the main door my hand slid into my trouser pocket and cradled the empty shampoo bottle that I had stolen from the bathroom earlier. I waited while the two of them walked ahead to the altar, which was surrounded by dozens of panels, each one showing a different biblical scene. Nathalie had told me that the altar itself was medieval. But I wasn't interested. I found what I was looking for almost at once. A font, close to the main door. And I was in luck. Just as I had hoped, it held a couple of inches of water.

Holy water. Do you get the idea? It was one thing that I knew a vampire couldn't stand. And there was no need to call my parents. If I was protected with a bottle of holy water, even a bottle that had once contained anti-dandruff shampoo, I would be safe. Making sure that nobody was watching, I managed to half-fill it, then replaced the lid and slipped it back into my pocket. I was feeling much more comfortable when, ten minutes later, we went back out into the cobbled courtyard and stood in the sun. The night could bring whatever it pleased. This time I was prepared.

In fact, the shadows were already stretch-ing out by the time we got back to the house, and it was only then that I began to have sec-ond thoughts. Perhaps I should have legged it for the airport after all. Right now I could have been in the air, on my way home. But you have to put yourself in my shoes. This was a vampire I was talking about. A vampire in the South of France! If I ran all the way home to England with an accusation like that and was then proved wrong, my parents would think I was crazy. I'd never live it down.

One way or another, I had to be sure.

Patrick was working late that night and we didn't eat until half-past eight. When I came up to the living room, there was no sign of Adrien. Nathalie was in the kitchen, putting the finishing touches to a *coq au vin*. And Vladimir was sitting in an armchair with some sort of leather-bound book balanced on his lap. I've already mentioned that one fea-ture of the living room was a spiral staircase. It stood to one side and twisted up to a gallery with bookshelves behind. Patrick had a desk up here and the gallery stretched the whole length of the room. It couldn't have been bet-ter. Making sure that nobody had seen me, I climbed quietly up and, keeping well back, continued along until I found myself directly above the reading man. The shampoo bottle was in my pocket.

Here, at last, was the final test. A tiny drop of holy water would mean nothing to an ordi-nary man. But to a vampire it would be like being stung by acid. It would burn his flesh – I'd seen it often enough in films. Being care-ful not to fumble, I took out the bottle and poured as little as I could into the cap. Then I reached out over the balcony. Vladimir Duclarc was directly below me. I turned my hand.

No more than two or three drops fell, but they hit him directly on the head. And that was when I knew, without any doubt at all, that I was right. Vladimir screamed and leapt out of his chair. The book tumbled to the floor. As Nathalie rushed across from the kitchen, he stood there, one hand pressed against his face. It was as if he was being burned alive. I couldn't believe that a minuscule amount of water could have such an effect. But of course, this wasn't ordinary water. And this wasn't an ordinary man.

Vladimir looked up angrily. I threw myself back, pressing my shoulders against the book-shelves. He couldn't see me. He couldn't possibly have guessed I was there. Natalie was next to him, dabbing at his skin with a tea towel. She was muttering to him – but even if she had been speaking in English I wouldn't have understood what she said. I stayed where I was, the bottle still in my hand. Eventually the two of them left the room, heading out into the garden, and I more or less tumbled back down the stairs. By way of an experi-ment, I dripped some of the holy water into my own hand. I felt nothing. It had no effect on me. But I wasn't a vampire. Not yet. Nor did I have any intention of becoming one.

I didn't go back to my room right then although as it turned out, everything would have been different if I had. I was feeling hot. The night was utterly still and seemed to be weighing down on me. I went out into the garden to get some air.

And that was when I saw them. Vladimir and Nathalie were kneeling close to the pool. He was splashing his face with non-sacred water. Neither of them heard me as I crept out behind them. But I heard them. And this time I understood at least part of what they said.

"Jack…" They were talking about me. "*Hier soir…*" Something about the night before. "*Le sang…*" That was definitely a word I knew. Vladimir had mentioned blood.

They talked for a couple of minutes. It was infuriating that I could only hear a few words of what they said and could only understand about half of those. But then came a sentence that rushed out of the darkness as if projected onto a screen.

"*Il doit être tué…*"

And that I did understand.

He must be killed.

Vladimir Duclarc spoke again.

"*Cette nuit…*"

Tonight.

What a fool I had been! I had managed to prove beyond any doubt that Vladimir Duclarc was indeed a vampire but in doing so I had exposed myself and left myself a prisoner in the house at the very worst time, after sunset, with at least six hours of darkness ahead. As I stood there, it seemed to me that the heat of the night had drained away and been replaced by an Arctic chill. I was on my own with them. There was no way out. And by the morning I would be dead – or worse. Suppose they turned me into one of them? What would it be like to live for a thousand years, condemned to hide in the shadows, feasting on the blood of other human beings?

Why had my parents sent me here? What

did French GCSE matter anyway? How had I let this happen to me?

There was a storm that night: one of those fat, heavy, spectacular storms that you only get in tropical climates when the heat of the summer becomes too much to bear. There was no wind, but the thunder was deafening, the lightning so fierce that it seemed to rip the whole world in two. The rain held off for as long as it could. Then it all came down at once, smashing into the house and turning the dry earth into livid, splattering mud. The wolves were howling too – at least, I thought I heard them. But it was the thunder that I remember most, great fists of it, slamming into the side of the house as if it wanted to smash down the walls.

I was awake. Even without the storm I wouldn't have slept a wink. I watched the shadows leaping across the room, the intense white light blasting against the brickwork, lingering for a few seconds and then disappearing as fast as it had come. Where were Adrien and the others? I had no idea. Crouching, miserably, on the bed, still fully dressed, I cursed my own stupidity. I should have left when I had the chance. There was nothing natural about this weather. Vladimir Duclarc had somehow summoned it up.

"*Il doit être tué…*"

He must be killed. Tonight. Before he can tell anyone what he knows. We will make him one of us and he will serve us for ever. Suddenly afraid, I reached out and turned on the lights. Nothing happened. The power supply had been cut. Of course. That would have been simple to arrange.

The door crashed open.

And there he was, on the other side. Vladimir Duclarc. He was wearing his black jacket. His long hair streamed behind him. His face, caught in another burst of lightning, had no colour at all, a snapshot from a cemetery. His eyes blazed. His mouth was open, his teeth glistening white. I knew he had come for me. I had been expecting it. But this time I was ready for him. "Go back to Hell!" I screamed. I had the shampoo bottle and I hurled the contents directly into his face, then followed them, hurling myself onto him.

There was only one way to get rid of a vampire. I had known what I had to do and, horrible though it was to contemplate, I had prepared myself.

The wooden stake had come from the garden. I had found it in a flowerbed and had sharpened it with a knife stolen from the dinner table. With all my strength, I rammed it into Vladimir Duclarc's chest, slanting down towards his heart. Another bolt of thunder struck at that precise moment. Vladimir screamed, but I heard nothing. The sound was drowned out by the elements. I pulled the stake out and struck a second time. I felt the point tear through his soft flesh. Blood, warm and red, spurted out, splashing into my face. I felt nauseous. But I had to be sure. One last time I ripped the stake out and then stabbed down again. This time I found his heart. I saw the light go out in his eyes. Blood, pints of it, gushed out of his mouth. He fell to his knees and I stood over him, knowing that in seconds he would crumble into ash.

Except that he didn't.

He was dead. That much was certain. I was drenched in his blood. There was blood all over the walls and floor. Then the lights blazed on. The return of the electricity was so sudden and the lights so bright that I was startled. I looked round. Patrick and Nathalie Duclarc were standing in the corridor, both wearing dressing gowns. Patrick was staring at me, his face filled with horror. Then his wife began to scream.

There is not much more to tell.

It seems that I was wrong about Vladimir Duclarc. He wasn't a vampire after all.

First of all, he came from Slovakia, which is nowhere near Transylvania. He had a little house in a place called Kežmarok where he worked as an antique's dealer, specializing in traditional Slovakian clothes, which he himself liked to wear.

What else can I tell you about him? Well, he didn't like garlic, but you already knew that. But it also turned out that he suffered from a condition called photophobia, which meant that he was extremely sensitive to light. He couldn't go out in the day without giving himself severe headaches and risking permanent damage to his eyes. Not surprisingly, perhaps, he felt very embarrassed about his condition and the family preferred not to mention it, although, of course, all in all it would have been better if they had.

Apparently he had come to my room that night because he was worried about me. According to Patrick Duclarc, the entire family had been a little concerned about my behaviour in the last few days. And they had thought I might be scared, on my own, in such a spectacular storm. Patrick and Nathalie had come downstairs a few seconds after Vladimir had opened the door. Both of them had witnessed the attack. Nathalie had needed to be sedated. It was Patrick who had called the police.

After I had murdered Monsieur Duclarc, I was driven down to the police station in Nice but I wasn't interviewed until the next day, when my parents arrived. Both of them looked completely shocked. They were accompanied by someone from the British Embassy, a man called Mr Asquith. They hadn't let me get changed yet. Apparently they still needed to take forensic evidence and I suppose I must have looked quite a sight, covered from head to toe in blood.

I told them about the way Vladimir had vanished by the gate and I also described what I had seen in the mirror. My parents didn't say very much to me. Mum cried a lot and Dad just kept on staring at me and shaking his head. Anyway, Mr Asquith went away for a few hours and when he came back he explained to me that there was actually a small door in the gate – I'd never noticed it – and that far from turning himself into a bat, Vladimir Duclarc had simply let himself out that way.

As for the mirror, that was the stupidest thing of all. I've already told you that it was on a door into a walk-in cupboard. Well, what I hadn't realized was that this door was covered in some sort of two-way glass. When the light was turned off inside the cupboard, the glass became a mirror. But when it was turned on, you could see right through it. When I'd seen Duclarc standing in front of the door on that sixth day, just before dinner, the light had been turned on. It was as simple as that. He had no reflection – and if I'd stood next to him, I wouldn't have had one either.

By now, I was feeling pretty sick, as I'm sure you can imagine. But there was still my last piece of evidence. "What about the holy water?" I demanded. It was a relief to be able to express myself in English. "I dropped a tiny bit of it onto Mr Duclarc and it burned him!"

But it seemed that the man from the embassy already had an answer to that. "The water you dropped went straight into Monsieur Duclarc's eye," he explained. "And it was in a shampoo bottle. It had got mixed with the shampoo that was still inside. Monsieur Duclarc had sensitive eyes anyway … as a result of his medical condition. No wonder he cried out in pain. The shampoo stung him quite badly."

"But I heard them talking about me!" I protested. "He said quite clearly that he was going to kill me."

It took a little longer to work that one out, but in the end we discovered that I was wrong about that too. Vladimir *had* been talking about me. He had been offering to give me a lesson in French and that was what I had heard. The French for lesson is *leçon* and not *le sang*, which sounds almost the same but means blood. As for the rest of it, I had misheard that too. He had been complimenting me on my grasp of the language…

He hadn't said,

"*Il doit être tué.*"

Which means: he must be killed.

But "*Il doit être doué.*"

Which means: he must be intelligent.

It was all a terrible misunderstanding.

I had to stay with the French police for a whole week but in the end I was allowed to return to England. But not home. My dad explained to me that, after what had happened, I wouldn't be able to come home for some time. Instead, I was sent to a sort of hospital called Fairfields. Actually, I might as well be honest. The sign outside reads: East Suffolk Maximum Security Hospital for the Criminally Insane.

And that's where I'm writing this. I'm hoping they won't keep me here much longer although it has already been one year. Mind you, my therapists tell me that I'm doing very well and, although they still give me lots of drugs, overall they're very pleased with my progress.

I've also, incidentally, taken my GCSEs since I've been here. And I'm delighted to tell you that my visit to Nice must have helped. Because, despite the rather unfortunate things that happened during my stay, I got an A* in French – so perhaps my father was right and the exchange was worthwhile after all.

She just hadn't expected it to happen to her...

SHEBAY

IT WAS WITHOUT DOUBT the most shocking thing she had ever heard.

"I'm sorry, Jenny, I really am." Her father was looking terrible. There were red rings around his eyes and he hadn't shaved. With his bald head, round chin and slightly protruding cheeks, he reminded her of one of those stocking-fillers she had once been given, the one where you use a magnet to drag iron filings onto a cartoon face. "You know things have been getting more and more difficult recently. This credit crunch. The business … all the problems we've been having."

"Your dad's done everything he could," her mother interjected. She had been crying. There was a tissue clamped in her right hand. Tears had turned it into a soggy mess.

"We've come to the end of the line," her father went on. "The banks won't cut me any more slack and, in a word, we're bankrupt. The house is going to have to go. And the car. I'm afraid the dog's going to have to be put down. And we can't keep you, either. You're going to have to be sold."

And that was it.

At first, Jennifer Bailey couldn't believe what she was hearing. She thought that she must still be asleep and she would wake up in a minute in her pink bed in her pink room and it would all have been a horrible dream. Of course she was aware that her parents were struggling. Her father had been working later and later every night, sometimes spending whole weekends at the office. There had been arguments and Jennifer had plugged herself in to her iPod with the volume turned up high to block them out.

Businesses had been going bust all over the country. She'd seen it on the news. But she had never believed it could be as bad as this.

Jonathan Bailey ran a garden-ornament business, selling fountains, furniture, bird-tables, gnomes and exotic plants to customers all over the south of England. He had invented some of the products himself. There was a bird-bath, for example, that actually had a small bird-shower attached. He had a radio-controlled gnome that sang highlights from Disney's *Snow White* and waved its arms in time to the music. And his range of garden furniture, manufactured from recycled wheelbarrows, couldn't have been more in tune with the times. What could possibly have gone wrong?

For twelve years, Jennifer had enjoyed an almost perfect life. She loved being an only child – it meant twice as much attention on birthdays and at Christmas – and she was never lonely. She adored her mother and she had a pet poodle – Boodle – who was allowed to sleep on her bed. She had a beautiful room in the family's three-storey home in Watford and she had even been allowed to decorate it herself, painting and draping everything in her favourite colour, pink. She went to an all-girls school just five minutes from the house where she was popular and successful, adored by her teachers and admired by her friends. In a recent vote to choose the new Head of School, she had come first by almost a hundred votes.

And now this!

"Can't you borrow more money?" she asked, with the wobble in her voice that usually meant she was about to burst into tears. But Jennifer forced herself not to cry. That would come later, when she was on her own.

Her father shook his head. "We're already

up to our ears in debt. Credit cards, mortgage, bank loan ... the lot." He sighed. "This is my fault..."

"Don't say that, Jonathan!" Jennifer's mother was a small, blonde-haired woman (although the colour now came out of a bottle). She was rather plump and always worried about her weight without ever actually doing anything about it. She also worked for the family business, doing the books. She and Jonathan had been married for seventeen years. "It wasn't your fault," she continued. "It's the market. They aren't interested in gardens any more."

"They're cutting back," Jonathan agreed. He shook his head. "I should never have bought those Tibetan prayer bells."

"The bells were lovely!"

"But nobody bought them. And we ordered ten thousand."

"It's too late for regrets." Jane Bailey turned to Jennifer. "There's nothing we can do," she said. She dabbed at her eyes with the useless tissue. Her mascara was halfway down her cheeks. "You're going to have to be strong, darling. We all are. But we can't look after you any more. Being sold is the best thing for you."

"But how are you going to sell me?" Jennifer asked and this time there was a crack in her voice and she felt the tears pressing against the backs of her eyes.

"We've already put you on sheBay," Jonathan replied.

Of course, it was obvious really. Once there had only been eBay – for objects of every description. But recently two more sites had been added to the World Wide Web: heBay for boys, and sheBay for girls. Jennifer knew well that these were difficult times. The newspapers never stopped going on about it – and anyway she'd seen it for herself. A dozen girls had been forced to leave school when their parents were no longer able to pay the fees. And at least half of them had been sold on sheBay in the family's last attempt to make ends meet.

She just hadn't expected it to happen to her.

"I think I'm going to go upstairs, if you don't mind, Mummy," she sniffed.

"Of course, precious," Jane said, struggling to keep her emotions under control.

"I'm sorry, Jenny," her father muttered. There was nothing else he could say. I'm sorry. I'm sorry. I'm sorry. What difference did it make? She was still going to be sold.

She climbed up to the first floor and went into her room, closing the door behind her. Curiously, she still didn't cry, even when she noticed Boodle sitting on the bed waiting for her. The poodle was wearing a pink ribbon and as usual was half-asleep, but when it saw her it wagged the short stump of its tail. The dog had no idea that in a few days' time it would be taken away for a lethal injection. Jennifer didn't bother patting it. Right now she had other things to worry about.

She sat down in front of the computer at her desk, tapped a few keys and went into sheBay, navigating her way to the page for members' accounts. Over the past year her parents had sold plenty of items over the internet, and although neither of them had said anything at the time, it was obvious now that they needed any money they could get. Jennifer knew their password on eBay. It was their surname backwards: YELIAB. Had they used the same word for sheBay? She typed in the six letters. The next page opened.

And there it was. Under ITEMS OFFERED her parents had posted several photographs of her, taken at her last birthday party, at school and walking on Hampstead Heath. She remembered her father taking that last shot. He had been very careful about it, framing her between two trees with the sunlight pouring over her shoulders. Had he already been thinking of using it for this purpose at the time? Jennifer felt anger rising. He'd pretended that it was to go on his bedside table. How could he have been so mean?

Her name was written under the photograph. A description followed.

JENNIFER JUDITH BAILEY

Age: 12 years 1 month
Height: 5'1"
Weight: 46 kilograms
Health: excellent

Jennifer is a delightful, intelligent girl with a friendly and pleasant personality. She has done consistently well at school — first in French and geography, second in maths, physics and biology. Her reports (available for inspection) are outstanding. In addition, she is a good cook and has kept a high level of fitness by playing tennis and lacrosse.

She would make an excellent servant or companion. Although a little shy, she has a reasonable grasp of world events and is a good conversationalist.

She is quick to learn and would soon adapt to new work. She is our only daughter and we are selling her with great reluctance. Offers starting at £1,000. Further enquiries to jrbailey@zmail.com.

The auction was to take place over the next forty-eight hours. So far there were three bidders. **SBEANSW3** had opened the bidding at the £1,000 demanded. Someone calling himself **drMACNEILceh** had raised it to £1,100. Twenty minutes later, **666grimsby** had gone to £1,300. The bidding was now back with **SBEANSW3** who had jumped to £2,000, perhaps trying to scare the others off. As for finding out who these people might be, there wasn't a great deal to go on but Jennifer was a bright girl and knew her way around the internet. In the next few hours she set to work, using a search engine – and common sense – to find out what she wanted.

SBEANSW3 was the first name she cracked. She guessed, correctly, that SW3 might be a London postcode, and by entering Bean and London into Google, she eventually came across a restaurant in Chelsea. Why would they be interested in buying a young girl? Their website provided the answer – and unfortunately it wasn't for the washing-up.

"Welcome to Sawney Bean restaurant in Cloak Lane, just off London's famous King's Road," it read, beneath a photograph of an old-fashioned building constructed of white-painted bricks. "Are you looking for the ultimate dining experience? Have you a special occasion that demands something very special indeed?

"We are London's only restaurant serving human flesh. Once a great delicacy in many parts of the world, 'long pig' (as it was known) was only recently reintroduced to European haute cuisine. High in vitamins and low in saturated fats, the delicately poached thigh of a young boy or girl will provide you with…"

Jennifer couldn't read any more. Her heart was in her throat and she wanted to scream or cry – or both! At the moment, **SBEANSW3** was ahead in the bidding. If the restaurant bought her, she would be killed and butchered and then poached! She would end up as the ultimate dining experience! How could her parents do this to her? Surely they wouldn't let it happen. But, as wretched as it was, Jennifer knew that £2,000 was a lot of money and they needed every penny they could get.

She turned her attention to **drMAC-NEILceh**. In her mind she imagined an elderly GP who had been unable to have any children of her own. Dr MacNeil would surely be a woman. Grey-haired and kindly. She was using her life savings to acquire a daughter.

But it turned out the truth was otherwise.

The initials **ceh** eventually led Jennifer to the Cambridge Experimental Hospital. Checking out their website, she found that Dr Roderick MacNeil headed its dissection unit. She had to look in a dictionary to find out what dissection meant.

"The action of cutting up an organism. The practice of performing surgical experiments upon animals such as frogs, rats or small girls."

The hospital's website told her everything she needed to know – and more. The Cambridge Experimental Hospital was at the forefront of medical science, not only finding new cures for old diseases but new diseases with no cures at all. The policy of the hospital was not to experiment on animals. This was considered cruel and, at the end of the day, unhelpful. Instead, the hospital regularly advertised for children and, indeed, there was a link to a page where you could offer sons, daughters, nephews and nieces for sale. Preferably they should be aged sixteen years or under and in excellent health.

Jennifer blinked. Even as she had been sitting at the screen, the bidding on sheBay had changed. **drMACNEILceh** had just raised the sum being offered to £2,250, putting him clearly in the lead. Jennifer's head was spinning. Was being used for medical experiments any better than being eaten for dinner? Either way she ended up dead. What was going on? She was a pretty, clever, adorable girl. Her mother had often told her so. She baked delicious sponge cakes and she could play one or two pieces by Chopin on the piano. Surely there must be someone out there who wanted her for herself.

She was unable to track down **666grimsby**. She knew that Grimsby was a town in the north and the three sixes did ring a faint – and unpleasant – bell in her head, but it was only the following morning, Saturday, that she had a stroke of luck. By then, **SBEANSW3** was back in the lead at an astonishing £3,000. Acting on impulse, Jennifer accessed her father's personal mailbox – and that was where she saw it. An email from 666:

> Can you let us have your
> daughter's zodiac sign?

Fortunately, Jonathan Bailey hadn't seen the email yet.

Jennifer typed back:

> Why do you want to know?

The answer came back almost at once:

> Blood sacrifice takes place on
> All Hallows' Eve (31 October).
> It helps to incorporate the
> child's star sign into the ritual.
> Sincerely, Ethan Kyte.

Jennifer thought she was going to be sick. First a restaurant for cannibals, then a hospital that wanted to cut her open for experiments and now a coven of witches! For that was what **666grimsby** undoubtedly was. The slightly unusual name – Ethan Kyte – led her to a website which only gave her more horrible details about what she already knew. Yorkshire had a long history of witchcraft and it seemed that the ancestors of certain fifteenth-century witches had regrouped and were using blood sacrifice and black-magic spells to raise powerful demons. 666 was, of course, the number of the devil. Their next "sabbat" – or secret meeting – was going to be in October. In his blog, Ethan Kyte wrote that he was actively looking for a young girl or boy to provide the necessary blood sacrifice.

There was absolutely nothing she could do. The sale was due to end on Sunday night and there were only these three bidders interested in her. That was when Jennifer did finally cry. Tears, hot and heavy, flowed down her cheeks and dripped off her chin. On the bed, Boodle began to whine. "Oh shut up!" she exclaimed. What did the dog know? It had an easy option compared with her.

Outside, the weather had turned gloomy as if reflecting her mood. The clouds had rolled in over Dandelion Close and the colour had drained out of the neat, square garden that her mother lovingly maintained. A single gnome stood near the gate, jerking its arms and humming, "Heigh–ho, heigh–ho…" she had always thought it adorable, but now she hated it. Why had her father ever dreamed up the stupid thing? Why couldn't he have started a business that actually worked?

During the course of the day, the bids climbed rapidly. By tea-time, Jennifer was worth £4,500 – which is what Ethan Kyte and his witches were prepared to pay to summon up the devil. Nobody else was interested. Jennifer was thinking of packing her bags and running away. She had nowhere to go and the police would probably find her and bring her back, but she had to do something! Maybe she could make it to the south coast. She could stow away on a ferry bound for France…

And then, just after six o'clock, a fourth bidder appeared.

The bid was £4,600 and the customer profile read **talltreesEastcott**. With a sense of excitement, Jennifer returned to Google. This one wasn't hard to track down. Eastcott was a village in Wiltshire, and Tall Trees had its own website.

Her heart leapt. An image had appeared on the screen of a beautiful country house in its own grounds. There were two people standing in front of it. They could have been anybody's grandparents, white-haired and smiling. Underneath them stretched a yellow ribbon and written on it in flowing letters were the words ORPHANAGE IN THE ENGLISH COUNTRYSIDE.

There was just one paragraph of text, but it told Jennifer everything she wanted to know.

"After travelling around the world, Gerald and Samantha Pettigrew founded the Tall Trees orphanage in 2001 with funds raised from private charities. They aim to provide a healthy, natural environment for orphans who might otherwise be exploited or even killed, taking in babies and young adults and caring for them on their extensive estate. Gerald and Samantha were both awarded the OBE in 2003 and have written extensively on matters relating to their work."

Jennifer felt a flood of relief. She wasn't an orphan – at least, not in the strictest sense of the word – but she was certainly being exploited and in danger of being killed. Quickly, she pulled up some pictures of Eastcott. Although it wasn't the prettiest of villages, it was situated in glorious countryside, right on the edge of Salisbury Plain. It had a village green and a handful of shops. Jennifer could already imagine herself growing up there. There would be other orphans. She would make new friends. And in time she would forget all about Watford and her parents.

But would the Pettigrews bid enough to save her? The auction was due to end on Sunday night at ten o'clock. It was now almost seven o'clock on Saturday and they were only one hundred pounds ahead of the competition. The bidding didn't change again, and at nine o'clock Jennifer was sent to bed. Her mother, still clutching a tissue, read her a bedtime story, but her eyes never left the book and when she kissed her daughter, she avoided her eyes. Jane Bailey was ashamed of herself. And, Jennifer thought, she had every reason to be.

Jennifer hardly slept at all that night. Once, at one in the morning, she got up and rebooted the computer; it only confirmed her worst fears. Dr MacNeil, the man who wanted to cut her up for medical experiments, was back in the lead at £5,000. The Pettigrews hadn't returned to the auction and Jennifer was certain they had forgotten her.

The next morning, at first light, she returned to the screen but nothing had changed. It was Sunday, her parents went to church as usual but Jennifer stayed behind, pretending she had flu. All day, she sat at her computer and watched as Dr MacNeil, Ethan Kyte and Sawney Bean fought over her. By the evening, it looked as if her future lay in haute cuisine … the London restaurant had raised the bidding to £7,500. At least the coven of witches had dropped out. After their £4,500 bid had been beaten, they hadn't bothered to come back. Presumably they would just have to find someone cheaper for their blood sacrifice.

At eight o'clock she was on the operating table.

At nine o'clock, with a price tag of £9,000, she was the main course.

Still nothing from the orphanage.

At twenty past nine, she was back under the dissecting knife.

The restaurant had one last try at half past nine. With thirty minutes until the end of bidding, he went to £9,500.

Dr MacNeil didn't respond.

Five minutes to ten. Jennifer had cried so much she thought she was empty, but even so more tears came from somewhere. She could imagine herself tied up in an oven. Maybe they would put an apple in her mouth. She just hoped she would give whoever ate her food poisoning.

And then, with one minute to spare, the miracle happened. The Pettigrews returned with an offer of £10,000. Jennifer could imagine her father gloating at that sum of money.

She had reached five figures! But that wasn't what she cared about. Surely this had to be the last word. The orphanage was taking her. Somehow they had found the necessary funds and she was going to be saved.

The minute hand on her Barbie alarm clock ticked to ten o'clock. The sheBay screen flashed red. The sale had closed. Gerald and Samantha Pettigrew of the Tall Trees orphanage in Wiltshire had won.

Things happened very quickly after that. Jonathan Bailey received a cheque in the post and went straight to the bank to cash it, while Jane Bailey packed her daughter's bags and bought her a single rail ticket to Pewsey. Apparently Eastcott was too small to have a station of its own. A few days later – once the cheque had cleared – a taxi came to the house to take her to Paddington, where she would board the train.

Her parents stood awkwardly by the front door.

"Well, goodbye, my dear," her father said. "Don't think too badly of us. We did try to be good parents."

"We did everything we could," Jane sobbed.

"Maybe things will go a bit better for us and one day we'll be able to buy you back…"

"I don't want to come back!" Jennifer cut in – and her voice was cold. "I don't ever want to see you again and I'll never forgive you for what you've done."

Her father went pale. Her mother began to cry all the harder.

"I'll have a much happier life without you, if you want the honest truth," Jennifer went on. "I always thought your garden business was stupid. And I hated living here. I'm really glad this has happened. I'd much rather be with the orphans than with you. I'm an orphan now myself. Goodbye!"

She got into the taxi and was swept away.

The journey to Pewsey took a little over an

hour. Jennifer had brought a book with her, but she spent most of the time looking out of the window, watching as the greyness and graffiti of London were replaced by the lush green of the English countryside. She wondered if there might be any other orphans on the train but although she went up and down the corridor a couple of times, she seemed to be the only child travelling alone.

Pewsey Station was delightful with its two long platforms, a single footbridge and neatly arranged tubs of flowers. Gerald and Samantha Pettigrew were waiting for her outside the ticket office and she liked them immediately. He was a short, round-shouldered man with a thick crop of untidy white hair, dressed in an old pin-stripe suit missing some of its buttons. Samantha was taller than her husband, wearing a loose dress and Wellington boots. She had a rather long nose with a thin pair of spectacles balanced half-way down. They were both smiling, both with a twinkle in their eyes, and they looked even sweeter and kinder than they had in their photograph. Jennifer was bursting with questions as they put her suitcases in the back of their car – a rather muddy Land Rover – and drove her through Pewsey and on towards Devizes.

"Is it far?"

"Not far now."

"Is there a swing in the garden?"

"Under the chestnut tree!"

"Do the orphans know I'm coming?"

"Oh yes. They're very excited."

They reached Salisbury Plain which sloped up, huge and empty, on their left. Ahead of them lay the village of Urchfont with its pretty duck pond and thatched cottages. The road twisted through open fields and centuries-old woodland, with Eastcott ahead of them, until at last they turned into the driveway of Tall Trees. And there it was, an old black-and-white manor house with oak beams and roses climbing up between the windows. The car

pulled up. The Pettigrews got out.

"Shall I bring my luggage?" Jennifer asked.

"No. Just come inside, dear," Mrs Pettigrew trilled. "We can see to all that later."

Jennifer hurried through the front door. Several things struck her at the same time. The house had very little furniture. The walls and the floor were bare. There was a strange smell in the air. And she could hear something, a sort of deep grumbling, coming from somewhere further inside.

"This way!" Mr Pettigrew exclaimed. He threw open a set of double doors. The grumbling became louder. In fact, it was more like growling.

"What is…?" Jennifer began.

But she had already seen what lay on the other side of the doors. There was a deep pit and, far below, a dozen animals were pacing back and forth, their vicious claws scratching against the straw-covered concrete, their eyes glowing hungrily, their bones rippling beneath their orange-and-black fur.

"Here they are!" Mrs Pettigrew waved a hand over the pit. "Our family of orphans."

"Orphans?" Jennifer quavered.

"Orphaned Bengal tigers," Mr Pettigrew explained. "Babies and young adults. It's terrible how they've been neglected. They would die if they were left on their own. But we look after them, Samantha and I. We let them roam in the grounds. We watch over them. And sometimes, as a special treat, we even give them fresh meat."

"But … but … but…" Jennifer began.

The Pettigrews grabbed hold of her. They were surprisingly strong. She felt herself being lifted off the ground.

"Feeding time!" Mrs Pettigrew exclaimed.

A moment later, Jennifer was hurtling through the air, diving head first towards the waiting pack below.

It was as if the massage chair
had become an electric chair in an American jail
and we were witnessing a horribly botched up execution...

ARE YOU SITTING COMFORTABLY?

I NEVER LIKED DENNIS Taylor, not from the start. I didn't like the way he dressed, with his blue blazer and silk cravat. I didn't like his moustache. I didn't like the way he laughed at his own jokes. But the very worst thing about him, the thing that made me squirm and wonder how I was going to survive the next ten years, was the fact that he was about to become my stepdad. How could Mum do this to me? Had she gone completely mad?

I had never known my father. He'd left home when I was very young and I never found out why. I'm sure my mum would have told me if I'd asked, but I never did. You may think that strange, but the truth is that the two of us were happy together. The life I had was the only one I knew. Why go digging up the past when all it will give you is dust in the eye?

We lived in a small house in Orford, which is right on the coast in Suffolk. There were only two bedrooms, but we didn't need any more as I didn't have any brothers or sisters – just a load of cats that came and went as they pleased. Mum worked part-time in a local hotel. She'd been left quite a bit of money by an eccentric aunt years back and she'd put it all in the bank for when she needed it. So although we weren't exactly rich, we weren't hard up either.

Mum was actually working at the hotel when she met Dennis. He was looking for a house in Orford ... he planned to move up from London. Well, one drink led to a chat, a chat led to lunch and soon they were seeing each other on a regular basis.

They got married at St Bartholomew's Church which was much too big and draughty for the little congregation that turned up. I was there with my best friend, Matt, and a handful of villagers. Mum's parents were still alive, but they lived in Scotland and she didn't invite them because she was afraid the journey would be too much for them. Dennis hadn't been married before. He produced a sister, who was plain and sulky, and a best man who apparently sold shares in the City. That was what Dennis did, by the way. Stocks and shares. He described himself as an *entrepreneur*. He liked sprinkling his language with French words.

After the service, they flew to Barbados for their honeymoon. Mum would have been happy just going to Cornwall or the Lake District, but Dennis persuaded her that they should do something more special. He also persuaded her – he was short of cash – to pay. I watched them leave, their car almost crashing into a white van as it turned the corner, coming the other way. At the time, I wondered if there was an omen in that. And in a way, as you will see, I was right.

I stayed with Matt and his parents while Mum and Dennis were away, and when they got back I was a little ashamed of myself for being so mean about it all. I was against Dennis. I hadn't wanted Mum to get married. I hadn't wanted them to go to Barbados. But here was Mum, sun-tanned and as happy as I'd ever remembered her. She'd bought me lots of presents, including earrings, a straw hat, a wrap, a carved wooden tortoise and all sorts of other stuff. She'd also taken hundreds of photos on a camera that Dennis had bought her at the duty-free. Seeing her like that, I made a resolution. I wasn't going to complain. I was going to adapt. I had a stepfather now. I was going to make him feel welcome.

It wasn't easy. Dennis didn't buy a house as he had planned. He simply moved into ours – which made sense because selling and buying would have been so expensive and anyway the market was pretty dead. I didn't say anything. It wasn't as if I was going to have to move out of my room or anything like that. But from that moment, everything changed.

You see, a house has a rhythm. The way people move around in it ... it's a bit like the workings of a clock. Suddenly, when I wanted to have a shower, Dennis would be there ahead of me. I couldn't wander around the kitchen in my knickers and T-shirt any more – I had to get dressed for breakfast. I felt uncomfortable watching TV in the evening. If Dennis and Mum were together in the living room, I felt almost like an intruder. And then there were unfamiliar smells and sounds. Dennis's aftershave. *Classic* FM blaring out of the radio every morning and Jeremy Paxman, religiously, every night. And Dennis's things lying around the place. The dirty clothes that he never put in the laundry bin. Curled-up cigarette ends (yes – he smoked) in the ashtrays.

I'll get used to it, I told myself. I tried to get used to it. Over the next few months I never complained. Christmas came and we had a pleasant enough time together. I had my GCSEs to think about. Mum still seemed happy, although I noticed she was working longer hours at the hotel. Apart from that, Dennis seemed to be looking after her OK.

I forget exactly when I began to realize that things were going wrong. I suppose money was the start of the slide downhill. Isn't it always? Dennis had sold his house in London, but after he'd paid off the mortgage he hardly got anything out of it. Also, his business wasn't going very well. I know that Mum had lent him money from her savings – she'd mentioned it to me – but of course the stock market had taken a dive and all of it had gone. I noticed that bills weren't being paid. There was a pile of them stuck in a corner of the kitchen. Some of them were printed in red ink. Final demands.

At the same time, Dennis was spending more and more. He'd bought himself a new car, a BMW which was parked on the street outside. There had also been other brief holidays – weekend breaks in Paris and Rome, at five-star hotels. I'm not saying my mum hadn't enjoyed these trips. But there was always the question of who was going to pay, and it followed her around like a cloud.

The biggest expense of all was Dennis's study. He needed somewhere to work, he said, so he had an ugly conservatory built at the back of the house and used it as an office. It completely spoiled the garden and it cost thousands – and worse still, there was a problem with the construction (he'd used builders

who had been recommended by one of his friends), so we had to spend thousands more putting it right.

My mum was paying for everything. She had never even been paid back for Barbados. I know because one morning they had an argument at the breakfast table. It came as quite a shock to hear their voices raised, and it made me wonder if there hadn't been other arguments when I was at school. or in whispers when I was asleep.

Mum had just opened a bill from a company that supplied fine wine. That was another of Dennis's extravagances. He loved expensive clarets. Some of the bottles cost twenty or thirty pounds.

"We can't pay this!" my mother exclaimed. She was staring at the bill, completely shocked.

"How much is it?" Dennis glanced at the total and raised an eyebrow.

"I really don't think you shouldn't have bought so much, Dennis. Not in the current climate. We'll have to send it back."

"We can't send it back."

"Why not?"

"It would make me look ridiculous. Anyway, I've already opened some of the bottles."

"But we can't afford it!"

Dennis scowled. "You really have no understanding of money, do you, Geraldine," he said. "It's true we're going through a bad patch. But I'm chasing one or two very interesting deals and everything will sort itself out in time. We just have to keep our nerve, that's all."

"But we've got dozens of bills…"

"Don't you trust me?" Dennis looked offended, but at the same time there was something else in his face, something I hadn't seen before. He looked threatening. "I've told you about this share opportunity in London. If it comes off…"

"But what if it doesn't?" My mother sat down and for a moment she looked close to tears. "We've gone through nearly all my savings in less than a year! I'm working extra hours…"

"I'm working too!"

"I know, dear. But sometimes I wish you'd work a little less. Your work is actually bankrupting us."

That evening, Dennis took us all out to dinner at the Golden Key to cheer us up. This was a smart pub in Snape, about five miles away. He ordered champagne and a nine-inch cigar. But when the bill came, I noticed he slid it over to my mum. "Left my credit card behind," he explained. "You get this, Geraldine. I'll pay you back."

He had to smoke the cigar outside on the terrace, and while he was gone I asked my mum if things really were as bad as they seemed.

"I don't know, Lucy," she said with a sigh.

"Has he really used all your savings?"

"I'm afraid so. He says you have to spend money to make money, but I don't think…" She broke off. "Don't you worry about this," she continued. She sounded completely worn out. "I'm sure it'll work out in the end."

"Are you still glad you married him?" I hadn't meant to be so direct but the words just slipped out.

"Of course!" she replied instantly.

I wasn't convinced. "You could always divorce him," I said.

Mum's eyes widened. I turned round. Dennis had come back into the dining room. He was standing right behind me and he must have heard what I had just said.

"Where's the cigar?" Mum asked. She looked really frightened. She was wondering if he had overheard our conversation.

"It made me feel sick," Dennis said. He reached for the car keys, which were lying on the table. "Let's go home."

None of us spoke on the way back. As soon as Dennis had parked his BMW, I hurried into the house and up to my room. I just wanted the evening to be over. But it wasn't yet. Not by a long way.

I'd just got into my pyjamas when my door opened and Dennis came in. I was quite startled to see him. He never usually came into my bedroom. He must have seen the expression on my face, because he smiled at me in that lazy way of his and said, "I just came in to say goodnight."

"Goodnight, Dennis," I said. I'd never called him Dad.

But he didn't leave. He sat down on the bed. "You know, I couldn't help overhearing what you said to your mum back in the restaurant," he drawled. "I'd hate to think you were turning her against me."

"I'm not," I replied.

"That's not how it sounded to me." He looked me straight in the eye. "In fact, young lady, I'd say you've been more or less against me from the start."

It's funny how things can change in an instant, like when the wind blows out a candle or a door swings open to show something horrible on the other side. That was how it was for me then. Dennis hadn't done anything or said anything particularly unpleasant. He was still sitting there in his smart blazer and grey trousers with one leg over his knee. But he was suddenly a completely different man and I realized two things in the same moment. I was scared of him. And he knew I was scared … it was what he wanted.

"I have to say," he went on, reasonably, "it would make life very difficult if you were my enemy. I'd have to think about separating you … sending you away to a boarding school."

"You can't afford boarding school," I said. I regretted the words as soon as I'd spoken them.

"We can sell this house. Get something smaller in Woodbridge or Leiston. Just your mother and me. Geraldine does what I tell her. You may have noticed that. You talk to her about me, she'll tell me – and you'll suffer the consequences." He stood up.

I flinched. For a moment I thought he was going to hit me. That was the power he had, a sort of animal quality. He had the upper hand and he knew it. He took one last look at me, then walked out of the room. I stayed where I was. I was trembling. That was the effect he'd had on me. And that was when I began to wonder. Was Mum afraid of him too?

In the next few weeks, Dennis's business affairs didn't get any better but he didn't seem to care. By now we had remortgaged the house. A home in Orford, even a tiny one like ours, was worth a lot of money. But the question was – how would we ever pay it back? As far as he was concerned, Mum was a virtually bottomless well and he could continue drawing on her until she'd been sucked dry. And then, just when I thought he couldn't be any greedier or any more demanding, up came the massage chair.

Dennis had seen it advertised in a magazine: the Silver City Pro-elite Massage System Deluxe. In the picture, it looked like something you might find at an up-market dentist's, a series of padded leather cushions on a swivelling steel frame, with headphones for the built-in MP3 player and two remote controls – one for massages, one for music. According to the advertisement, the SCPMSD came with state-of-the-art roller-and-airbag technology, a powerful (but silent) tri-point hydraulic system and a choice of fifteen different programs as well as a unique Body Memory feature which automatically took your weight and measurements and selected the massage to suit your needs. Other bonuses included a super-strong air-pressure option, a full-colour LCD, economy standby mode and automatic shut-off. The SCPMSD was being offered at a special, once-only price of £3,950 + VAT.

"We're simply not getting this," Mum said, pushing away the advertisement which Dennis had thrust under her nose.

"But it's my birthday!" Dennis scowled. In fact, his birthday was still a month away.

"I'd love to get it for you. But I simply can't. There's no money in the bank and my credit cards are all over their limit."

"We can get another credit card."

"Why do you need a massage chair?" Mum asked.

Dennis rubbed his neck. "Living with the two of you, always criticizing me all the time! You have no idea how stressed I am. If I was more relaxed, I'd be able to concentrate on my business a little more."

"I'm sorry, Dennis. I'm sure it would be a lovely thing to have. But I'm afraid this time what you're asking really is out of the question."

The massage chair turned up a few days later. It was a monstrous thing that took four men to carry in, and by the time it had been installed in the living room, there was hardly any space for anything else. Dennis wasn't there when it arrived. He was at the pub, somewhere he'd been spending more and more time recently. After the delivery men had finished their work and gone, I found Mum in the kitchen. I could tell that she'd been crying.

"Mum!" I went over to her and this time I wasn't going to hold back. "Why are you putting up with this?" I demanded. "It's stupid. You should get rid of him. You should kick him out."

"Sssh!" She turned round and for a moment she looked terrified. "You don't understand, Lucy. I can't…"

"Has he threatened you?"

"No. It's not like that."

"Then why?"

I heard the front door open and my heart sank.

"He's not so bad," my mum whispered.

"And maybe he'll be happy … now that he's got his chair."

In fact, Dennis was delighted. He sat in it at once and began to experiment with the programs, trying to find the one that suited him best.

Have you ever seen a massage chair? For something that was meant to be a luxury item, this one was really hideous. The leather was black and highly polished, and even if it was packed with the latest technology, it still looked awkward and old-fashioned. It was also very big, completely enclosing Dennis when he sank into it … a bit like a mummy in its sarcophagus. The chair sat on a metal plinth. There were supports for his arms and legs, and when the program started, these gently pressed on both sides of his wrists and ankles, massaging them and at the same time keeping him in the correct position. Cushions also inflated behind his head and around his neck and hidden rollers moved up and down his spine, under his hips and thighs and even behind his calves. Every inch of his body was catered for and, just as the advertisement had stated, the massage chair was practically silent, with only a faint humming as it went about its work.

I hated that chair. You have to remember that we lived in a small, pretty house and the chair – with its pistons and rollers and airbags and leg traction – completely spoiled it for me. I could always tell when it was on. I couldn't hear it but the walls of my bedroom vibrated. I thought of it as a monster in a cave. If any of our friends had seen it, they would have said it was completely out of place, better suited to an airport lounge or health club. But not many friends visited us any more. (They didn't much like Dennis either.)

Dennis had the chair for less than a week before it broke down. He used it every evening. He had a set pattern: after dinner, he'd pour himself a glass of expensive wine, light one of his expensive cigars and sit there in his black leather beast with a vague smile on his face, watching TV. Meanwhile, Mum would do the washing-up and maybe the ironing before she went to bed, and I'd stay in my room, doing my homework, almost afraid to go out.

Well, one evening, just before I went upstairs, he got himself all set up, reached for the remote control, pressed down with his thumb and…

Nothing happened.

"Geraldine? Have you been tampering with this?" he demanded.

"No." My mum stopped, a pile of washing in her arms.

He tried again. "It's not working."

"Is it plugged in?" Mum asked.

"Of course it's plugged in, you stupid woman. You can see for yourself. The green light is on."

"Well, it's not working."

"I know it's not working. I just said that."

"Maybe it's fused," I suggested, secretly hoping it was something more serious.

"We need to call someone in," Dennis said.

"I'll find someone," my mum said. She was really upset. I don't suppose she cared about the stupid chair, but she didn't want Dennis to be in a bad mood.

She rang the chair company the following morning – but that prompted the next crisis. The Silver City Pro-elite Massage System Deluxe was still under guarantee, but Dennis had lost the paperwork and they said they wouldn't come to the house if we didn't have it.

"We can get someone local," I said. "I bet it's something simple. Maybe one of those stupid pistons has fallen off or something."

"Lucy!" My mother rolled her eyes nervously, even though Dennis wasn't in the house.

"I'll find a number," I said.

I went into the kitchen. The Yellow Pages telephone book was lying open on the windowsill next to the sink – and here's the strange thing. As I walked over to it, there must have been some sort of breeze in the room, because the pages fluttered and turned as if the telephone book were opening itself. Stranger still, by the time I reached it, it had settled in exactly the right place, because there was an advertisement in a black box in the top corner that drew my eye immediately.

THE MECHANIC
General household repairs.
Electrical, plumbing,
computer hardware, domestic.
Tel: 00010 005 500
We fix everything.

I showed the advertisement to Mum and she rang the number, although she was a little puzzled by all those zeroes. What sort of phone had a number like that? I'm not sure she was even expecting to get an answer, but she was connected after the first ring. She spoke briefly to someone at the other end of the line, then put the phone down. "They're coming on Saturday," she said.

"Are they expensive?" I asked. I was always worrying about money these days even if it was the one subject we never talked about.

"They didn't say." Mum saw the look in my eyes. "However much it is, it'll be worth it," she said. "Dennis loves that chair. And it does help keep him calm."

The mechanic turned up at ten o'clock the following Saturday, exactly when he'd said he would. He came in a white van that reminded me of something. Had I seen it before, on the day of the wedding? If so, it was a strange coincidence. In any event, he entered the house carrying a neat, metal toolbox. He

was a very short man, barely taller than me, dressed in blue overalls with a biro behind his ear. At first sight, I thought he might not be British. He was dark-skinned, bald, with a moustache that was a little too big for his face. His teeth were a dazzling white. All in all, he didn't look like a mechanic. He looked like someone dressed up as a mechanic.

Dennis had just finished breakfast and followed the mechanic into the living room. The little man was already crouching in front of the chair.

"What a beauty!" he was saying. "The Silver City Pro-elite Deluxe! Multi-airbag system. Twin 26-point shiatsu rollers! I congratulate you, sir, on your good taste. Only the best for you. I can see that!" He straightened up. "I bet you must love sitting on this."

"It doesn't work," Dennis said.

"That's the trouble with Silver City." The mechanic shook his head. "They're unreliable. It's Japanese engineering. Not that I've got anything against the Japanese. Great cars. Great TVs. But when it comes to massage chairs, they can be a bit shoddy, a bit slapdash…"

"Can you fix it?" Dennis asked.

"I can fix anything. It might take an hour. It might take all day. We won't know that until we've got the back panel off and I've had a quick scout around inside."

"How much will it cost?" Mum asked.

"Fifty pounds plus VAT or forty pounds cash."

I could see Mum was relieved. We'd had plumbers and electricians come to the house and they'd charged double that just to walk through the door.

"Mind you," the mechanic went on. "Let's hope the vertical sensors or the spine rotation systems haven't blown. That could be more expensive. And I might have to take out the motherboard. This Japanese circuitry … it can play all sorts of tricks."

"Just mend it," Dennis said. "I'm going out." Dennis had recently taken up golf. Mum had used her connections at the hotel to get him cut-price membership at a local club.

As soon as he had gone, the mechanic set to work. He opened his toolbox to reveal a gleaming array of spanners on the top shelf with a dozen screwdrivers, pliers, wrenches and tweezers neatly lined up below.

"Would you like some tea?" Mum asked.

"No, thank you, Geraldine," the mechanic replied. "But I wouldn't mind a glass of water. Tap, not mineral. And maybe a slice of lemon?"

"Right…" My mum sounded bewildered.

And there was something that puzzled me. I had been there when she had made the telephone call and I had been there when the mechanic arrived. Mum had never told him her name. He couldn't possibly have known it.

But he had called her Geraldine.

The next time I looked into the living room, the massage chair had been turned inside out. The mechanic had taken off the leather cushions to reveal a metal panel which he had unscrewed. Now there were about a thousand wires spilling onto the carpet and I could see metal pistons, cogs, wheels and circuit boards packed together inside. The mechanic was whistling cheerfully but my heart sank. I'd decided that he was a complete fraud. I didn't believe for a minute that he had the faintest idea what he was doing.

I was wrong. He worked for three hours, occasionally stopping to sip the lemon-flavoured tap water he had requested. When I went into the room again, the chair had been put back together again and looked as good as new. He was just screwing the panel back into place.

"Is it fixed?" I asked. It was the first time I had spoken to him.

"As right as rain, Lucy. Fixed and fastened."

"How do you know my name?"

"Your stepfather told me." He slipped another screw into place and began to turn it.

"Do you live in Suffolk?" I asked him.

"No, no, no. Not me."

"So where do you live?"

"I get around."

At that moment, my mum came into the room. She took one look at the chair and I could see the relief in her face.

"It was the auxiliary sprocket," the mechanic told her. "Would you believe that someone had put it in upside-down! It short-circuited the main drive. And without the main drive the whole thing was a non-starter." He picked up the remote control and pressed a button. The massage chair began to vibrate the way it always had. Music played in the headphones. The back rollers gently pulsated. Everything seemed to be working.

"How much do I owe you?" my mother asked.

"Forty pounds if you don't mind paying cash," the mechanic replied.

"But you've been here for hours," Mum said.

"Yes. It took a little longer than expected. But the price I quote is the price you pay. And forty pounds it is!"

"Well … thank you very much." Mum reached for her handbag and took out two twenty pound notes.

The mechanic rolled them up like a cigarette and slipped them into his top pocket. "It's been a pleasure meeting you," he said. "And a pleasure working on the Silver City Pro-elite. What a chair! What a great invest-ment! I wish you hours of pleasure. Good day!" He had already packed up his toolbox. He picked it up and left.

Dennis was in a bad mood when he got back from the golf club, which meant that he had lost. But he brightened up a bit when he saw the massage chair. "Is it mended?" he asked.

"Yes, Dennis," my mum said.

"Did that man demonstrate it before he left?"

"He turned it on."

"Did he run through all the programs?"

"Well, not all of them…"

"You shouldn't have let him leave without going through all the programs," Dennis said. "If he's damaged it…"

"It seemed to be working all right."

"We'll see!"

Dennis didn't actually try the chair until after dinner. As Mum and I cleared the table, he lit a cigar, poured himself a glass of wine and ambled into the living room. I heard the squeak of the cushions as he sat down. Then came the faint *tish-tish-tish* of music being played through the headphones. A moment later, the chair – and much of the house – began to vibrate.

"Well, that seems to be all right," my mum said.

"Let me make you a coffee," I said. Mum was looking exhausted.

"Thank you, Lucy. That would be nice."

How long did it take for everything to go wrong? I can't tell you. Even now I find it hard to remember exactly what happened. Maybe I don't want to. My therapist told me that sometimes, without even trying, we block out things too horrible to recall. Not that I'm seeing a therapist any more. But she might have been right.

"Geraldine!" It was Dennis calling my mum. Already there was something in his voice. He didn't just want another glass of wine or an ashtray for his cigar. It wasn't just that he'd forgotten his reading glasses. Something had gone wrong.

My mum put down the pan she'd been drying.

"Geraldine!" His voice was louder, more

high-pitched. And there was something else. The sound of the chair had intensified. The walls of the kitchen were vibrating more violently. A plate trembled its way to the edge of the counter, fell to the floor and smashed.

Together, Mum and I ran into the living room.

At first, it looked as if Dennis was clutching the massage chair with all his strength, but we saw quickly that he was actually trying to escape from it. But he couldn't. The wrist and ankle pads which were meant to hold him gently in position had over-inflated, effectively pinning him down. His fingers were writhing but he couldn't release his arms. At the same time, his entire body was convulsing as it was pummelled by pistons and rollers which were hopelessly out of control. They were battering him! I couldn't believe what I was seeing. It was as if the massage chair had become an electric chair in an American jail and we were witnessing a horribly botched-up execution.

"Let me … aaaaagh!" Dennis screamed but we could barely hear him. The headphones were still sitting lopsidedly on his head but the volume control must have broken because we could actually hear the bass and the drumbeat filling the room, impossibly loud. *TISH-TISH-TISH.* What it must have been like for Dennis with the speakers clamped over his ears was impossible to imagine – and then I didn't need to imagine it because a second later one of his eyes exploded like a wet balloon.

My mum screamed, then ran forward and snatched up the remote control. Dennis had dropped it on the carpet. I saw her thumb stab down on the STOP button, again and again. But the chair didn't stop. It had hardly even begun. Dennis was jerking about like a mad thing, his wrists and ankles still pinned down and his chest and thighs heaving. Blood was pouring out of his nose. His fingers were writhing. And he was still screaming, the words incoherent now. The pain was stretching his face in every direction so that I hardly recognized him.

I had to do something. But what? I was terrified. I didn't want to go near the massage chair. But I couldn't just stand there and let it kill him. Suddenly I had an idea. I ran over to the wall and ripped out the plug.

The massage chair picked up speed.

How could that be? Did it have a secondary power source? Or had it somehow stored up enough energy to continue its hideous destruction? The twin 26-point shiatsu rollers underneath Dennis's legs surged forward and I heard his bones break. All of them. They were unable to withstand the pressure. Then it was his ribs, snapping one at a time as the tri-point hydraulic system slammed into him again and again.

"Unplug it!" Mum screamed at me.

"I have!" I screamed back.

It was already too late for Dennis. I'm not even sure he was still conscious. The massage chair was shuddering and shaking as if it was trying to leave the room and he was being thrown from side to side with all sorts of disgusting fluids splattering across the furniture. And then, finally, it had to happen. The quadruple rollers behind his head, the ones that promised the best spine massage ever, locked together with ferocious strength. Dennis's neck broke with a snapping sound like a branch of a tree. The machine stopped.

Silence filled the room.

Gently, the air bags deflated, allowing Dennis to slump forward so that now he looked asleep … if you could ignore his twisted frame and all the blood oozing out of him. The music had stopped. Smoke was trickling out of his ears. The chair itself looked worn out, ready for the scrap heap. Somewhere inside it a final spring snapped with a faint twang.

I thought my mum would be in hysterics, but she was surprisingly calm. "Lucy," she said.

"Leave the room."

"Yes, Mum."

"We'll call an ambulance from the kitchen."

"Yes, Mum."

"And the police."

There's not very much more to tell.

The police investigated, of course. They were particularly keen to speak to the mechanic, the man who had supposedly fixed the massage chair. It was still unclear how the machinery could have malfunctioned in such a remarkable way. The chair was taken to pieces by forensic scientists. The software and electronics were minutely examined. But no one was left any the wiser.

And the mechanic had disappeared. There was still the number in the telephone book, but when the police tried it, there was no reply. It wasn't that the number had been disconnected. According to the telephone company, it had never existed in the first place and for a short while the finger of suspicion pointed to my mum. Could she have deliberately sabotaged the massage chair to murder Dennis? Even the police had to admit that the idea was ridiculous. She had no engineering knowledge. And as far as the outside world was concerned, she had no reason to want to kill her husband.

Even so, the complete disappearance of the mechanic was a mystery, particularly as he could most certainly have helped the police with their enquiries.

In the weeks that followed, there were a couple of pleasant surprises. First of all, Dennis had a small life-insurance policy which paid out following his death. But much more significantly, Silver City, the manufacturers of the Pro-elite massage chair, got in touch with my mum. They had heard what had happened and were very anxious that they were going to get the blame. Dennis's horrible death could ruin their business if it were made public …

and Mum could easily sue them. So some lawyers came to see her and in the end, to apologize for her distress – and to keep her quiet – they wrote her a cheque. I was there when she opened it. It was a six-figure sum.

I saw the mechanic one more time.

A year had passed. Mum and I were still living in the same house in Orford, although we'd now had the conservatory removed. Mum had gone back to working just three days a week and I was in the middle of my GCSEs. It was a beautiful day with a huge summer sun high in the cloudless sky. We'd just been shopping in Woodbridge and were on our way back to the car. We'd swapped the BMW for a new car, something smaller and less fancy that better suited our needs.

And that was when I saw a white van tearing down the street, perhaps on its way to someone else's house. I even got a glimpse of the mechanic, behind the steering wheel, with his bald head and moustache. And although I may have imagined it, I could have sworn he turned towards me and winked.

A moment later he had turned the corner and gone, and the last thing I saw were the words written on the side of his van.

THE MECHANIC

And, just below that:

We fix everything.

And I had to admit that, in his own way, he had.

"I expected you to come..."

PLUGGED IN

HE WAS SUCH A NICE boy. Everyone in his family agreed. He was the sort of boy you could be proud of, who would get a dozen A*s and go to the best university, who would have a wonderful career and would look after his parents when they were old. An only son, of course. There's no one more devoted than an only child … maybe it helps that there are no brothers or sisters to fight with. Not that Jeremy would ever have fought with anyone. Every evening he helped wash the dishes without being asked. He walked the dog without complaining. Other parents might sit worrying about drugs and cigarettes and nightclubs full of predatory girls. But Jeremy Browne seemed untouched by the modern world. He was impervious to it. He was the sort of boy Enid Blyton might have written about – the Famous Five, the Sensational Six or maybe just the Wonderful One.

He lived in Finchley, in North London … in a large, Victorian house on Elmsworth Avenue which had once been rather grand but which, like many of the houses around it, had been converted into flats. The Browne family had the bottom floor with a bright and airy basement and a garden. Jeremy liked to help with the gardening too. His father was the local manager of a well-known building society. His mother taught at a primary school just behind Finchley Central tube station. Mike and Irene Browne had arrived at parenthood fairly late in life – indeed, Jeremy had come as a complete surprise … though a wonderful one, of course. The three of them were often seen shopping together, at church, or strolling on Hampstead Heath with their dog, Scampi – a mongrel that had once been rescued by the RSPCA – racing ahead of them.

Jeremy was unusual in that he was academically gifted, physically remarkable and athletically an all-round sportsman. He was a very handsome boy with long, fair hair, blue eyes and the sort of smile you'd notice across a room. By the time he was fifteen, he had begun to fill out. He was already taller than his mother, and with his broad shoulders, thick neck and general air of confidence he could easily have been mistaken for an American football player. He loved sport. He played for his school football team, did rugby training most weekends and had even considered professional ice-skating … there was a rink at Alexandra Palace, not far away.

There were, it has to be said, a few people who thought that Jeremy was just too good to be true. He was not the most popular boy in the school. Many of the other children mistrusted him and some threw hurtful insults his way. Even some of the teachers had their doubts. To be passionate about the poetry of William Blake was fine … but at the age of twelve? And then there was that tricky moment when he tried to convert his maths teacher to Christianity. JEREMY BROWNE IS GAY read the graffiti on the side of the nearest bus shelter and sadly this was one of the kinder things that had been written about him.

And it would have been no surprise either that it was Jeremy who volunteered to drop in on the new neighbour who had just moved into Elmsworth Avenue. The very last house in the street was also the smallest and the shabbiest and had, for some time, caused concern among the other residents. The square of grass that was the front garden had become overgrown. The dustbins were overfilled with bottles, old newspapers and plastic supermarket bags filled with rubbish. No recycling here! The windows were dusty and the roof was in disrepair. But fortunately the last occupant had left, and now the house had been rented out again.

It was often said that this area of London was a particularly friendly one and more like a village, really, than a major suburb. Everyone looked out for one another, whether it was via the Neighbourhood Watch scheme or just a quick gossip over the garden fence. And so it was that word began to spread about the new arrival. He was an elderly man, single and a foreigner – from Poland or perhaps Hungary. There were some who said he had been a hero of the Second World War, although that would make him at least ninety. Another report suggested that he was actually a retired nobleman – a grand prince or a duke. His name? The postman, who chatted to everyone on his round, quickly revealed that it was Jákob Demszky. This was the one certainty. Everything else was rumour. He was a widower. He had come to England for his health. He might even have been born here and had come home to die.

The removal van had come and gone very quickly. It was obvious that Mr Demszky did not have much in the way of furniture or personal possessions. Since his arrival, he had been spotted a couple of times, once making his way home with a shopping basket in one hand and a walking-stick in the other, once pottering about outside the house, trying to clear a drain.

He was a tiny man in a dark, old-fashioned suit with a coat hanging off his shoulders so that he was a bit like bat man … not the comic hero but a sad, dusty creature that might be found in an abandoned castle or church. He walked slowly and with difficulty. Indeed, any movement seemed to give him pain. His shoes were well polished and he wore two gold rings on the fingers of his left hand. One of them contained a jewel which sparkled, blood-red, in the North London sun. His walking-stick was topped by a silver ram's head, the horns curling into the palm of his hand.

"You know, I think I ought to go and see him," Jeremy announced one Saturday, at breakfast.

"That's very thoughtful of you, Jeremy," his father said over a spoonful of organic muesli.

"He must be finding it very strange," Jeremy continued. "Apparently he doesn't speak much English. And there's tons of work to do at that house."

"Why don't you take him round a slice of my home-made treacle tart?" Jeremy's mother suggested. "I could wrap it in silver foil…"

Very soon afterwards, Jeremy found himself clutching a large wedge of tart and knocking on the door of 66 Elmsworth Avenue (the bell seemed to be out of order). It took Mr Demszky a long time to answer it, and Jeremy could imagine him lifting himself painfully out of his chair and shuffling along the corridor… But eventually the door swung open and there he was, staring out with eyes that were both politely enquiring and a little nervous.

"Yes?"

"Hello. My name is Jeremy Browne. I live at number 50. I was wondering if there was anything I could do to help you." Jeremy lifted his package. "And my mother thought you might like a slice of her home-made treacle tart."

Mr Demszky considered all this as if trying to make sense of it. Then a soft, happy smile spread across his face. "How very kind! Please, come in…"

Jeremy followed the old man through a darkened hallway and into the kitchen, which seemed bare and empty, with just a few food supplies and a couple of chipped mugs on the Formica surface. He had already realized that Mr Demszky spoke better English than he had been told, though with a heavy accent. The man really was very small indeed, as if he had shrunk into himself over the years. His skin was completely grey, with dark liver spots on his neck and the side of his head. His hair was white, curling limply down over the collar of his jacket. His fingers were long and mis-shapen, with yellowy nails that were somehow more animal than human. But most unnerv-ing of all were his eyes. They were colourless and bulged slightly out of his face, like two plastic sachets filled with water. He grunted as he sat down. There were gaps between his teeth and Jeremy could see his tongue, as grey as the rest of him, flickering behind them.

"Would you like some tea?" Mr Demszky asked.

"Let me make it for you," Jeremy said. That was his way. He had come here to help, and he certainly wouldn't let the old man make any effort for him.

"No, no. I already had…" When Mr Demszky spoke, his voice was partly trapped in his chest. He had to force the words and they came out in a wheeze. "What did you say was your name?"

"It's Jeremy Browne."

"How old are you, Jeremy Browne?"

"I'm fifteen."

"That is a good age. That is a very lovely age."

Despite himself, Jeremy was feeling a lit-tle uncomfortable. The old man was staring at him in a most peculiar way, as if he had never seen a boy before, and he was trembling as if the journey to the door had almost been too much for him. "Is there anything I can do here to help you?" he asked.

"You are so very kind!" Mr Demszky nod-ded so vigorously that Jeremy heard the bones in his neck creak. "I expected you to come. Yes. But so soon? So soon?" He paused for breath. "You could perhaps do a little garden-ing?" He spread his hands. "There are dead leaves. Dead plants. So much that is dead. Have you the time to help me in the garden? I will pay you…"

"I don't need paying," Jeremy said. "Just show me what you want me to do."

Jeremy worked for three hours that day. And he returned the following Wednesday and did three more hours. This time his mother came with him, and after meeting Mr Demszky she took the opportunity to spring-clean much of the house, and even invited the old man to join them for dinner the following week. Although Jeremy wouldn't have admit-ted it, he was a little uneasy inside number 66. The house was dark and musty and smelled of something he couldn't quite place. He hadn't wanted to pry, but he couldn't help noticing that many of the doors were locked. He had been unable to go into the study, for exam-ple, and also the curtains in that room were drawn so he couldn't look in from outside. In any event, he felt more comfortable out in the fresh air, so he had set to work clearing out the garden shed which was full of rubbish, some of it quite possibly hazardous. His father had already volunteered to drive it down to the local skip.

Jákob Demszky did come to dinner – and he brought gifts for the entire family. Hungarian wine for Mike, and flowers for Irene. But for Jeremy he had something rather special. He took out a black cardboard box tied with a black ribbon and slid it across the table.

Lying there, it reminded Jeremy of a mini-ature coffin and for a moment he was unsure whether to open it. "What is it?" he asked.

"Unwrap it," Mr Demszky said.

"Go on, Jeremy." His father laughed. "It won't bite you."

Jeremy picked up the box, slid off the

ribbon and opened it. From the weight, he had been expecting a pen or perhaps a multi-purpose knife, and he was surprised to find himself holding an MP3 player … although it wasn't like any MP3 player he had ever seen before. It wasn't an iPod or anything modern. In fact it wasn't branded at all. It was just a rectangular block of plastic, flat and chunky, with a glass window and a few controls.

"It is for you," Mr Demszky said. "To thank you for your help."

The MP3 player was obviously a Hungarian model, for when Jeremy switched it on a series of strange words floated across the screen: TÉPÕFARKAS … GONOSZUL … AKTÍV.

"What does that mean?" Jeremy asked.

"It's warming up," Mr Demszky explained.

"Why don't you give it a try?" Irene said.

Jeremy picked up the machine. The ear-plugs looked too big for him with wires as thick as spaghetti and he wondered if it would even work and – if it did – what it would play. But when he plugged it in, he was surprised to discover that Mr Demszky had already down-loaded several tracks by his favourite bands: Coldplay and The Killers. More than that, the quality of the MP3 player was amazing. The music poured into his head in a torrent, sweeping away the dining room, the tick of the grandfather clock, the entire world. Every lyric, every note was crystal clear. It was as if he had been transported to the front row of the O2 arena. He was actually sorry when his mother served the first course and he had to switch it off again.

The evening was a huge success. Mrs Browne had cooked lasagne, her signature dish, and although Mr Demszky hardly ate anything, he talked at length about his life in Hungary. It turned out that he had once owned a castle near Budapest and for fifty years has been one of the country's most celebrated scholars. He had lectured in astrology, psychiatry and medieval history. He had

actually been the head of a society that had been formed in the Middle Ages and which still met on certain days of the year to discuss philosophical issues. There had to be a full moon, Mr Demszky explained. Otherwise, the members – the BOSZORKÁNYS, as he called them – would not come out.

"And what are you doing in England?" Mrs Browne asked.

Mr Demszky paused for a moment. He looked from his plate to Mrs Browne and then from her to her son. "I came to meet people like you," he said.

In the weeks that followed, the Brownes saw a lot of their new neighbour, helping him in small ways or just popping in to see that he was all right. And Jeremy never walked up the road without his new MP3 player plugged into his ears. It was incredible. Not only did it have his two favourite bands, but all the other music that he loved somehow found its way into the machine, as if arriving there over-night. Three days before Take That released their new single, it magically appeared on his playlist. It seemed he only had to think of a tune and he would find it … without even having to pay. And there was something else rather strange. The MP3 player didn't seem to have a battery compartment. In fact there were no plastic panels or visible screws at all. It was moulded together with just the sin-gle socket for the jack plug at the end of the earplugs, and the switches to start the whole thing up. He vaguely wondered if it might be solar-powered – but that was ridiculous. Solar-powered MP3 players didn't exist.

But it never slowed down or stopped. For the first time in his life, Jeremy got into trou-ble at school. MP3 players weren't allowed, but Jeremy couldn't resist plugging himself in between lessons, out in the yard, and he found himself dreaming about the music during les-sons, ignoring whatever the teachers said. He wore it to and from school and kept it on in his room when he was doing his homework. He still went round to Mr Demszky's from time to time – the garden was beginning to look delightful – and he worked all the harder with the music enveloping him, transporting him into its own world. Beyoncé, Oasis, Kings of Leon … the new tracks kept arriving and Jeremy kept on listening. At night, in bed, he still read books but he did so to the rhythms of Leona Lewis or Estelle and his parents became familiar with the *tish-tata-tish-tata-tish* sounds that came from their son every morning at the breakfast table.

They became a little concerned. Like many other teenagers, Jeremy had begun to communicate less and less … but until now he had never been like other teenagers. He had been special. What had happened? All he did was listen to that wretched music. Irene Browne was the first to mention it. They didn't talk to one another as a family any more, she said. She even began to think that meeting their neighbour might not have been such a good thing after all. He seemed to have snatched something of her son away, and she suggested to her husband that maybe it would be a good idea to remove the MP3 player, to give Jeremy a rest. But before either of the Brownes could act, something else happened which completely took their minds off modern music and earplugs. Jeremy became ill.

It was hard to tell when it began. Maybe it was about two weeks after Mr Demszky had moved in, but on the other hand it could have actually started before he arrived. It appeared, initially, to be a sort of virus. Jeremy was tired all the time. He found it hard to get up and, in the evening, he went back to bed as soon as he could. He still had an appetite but he didn't enjoy his food, eating it mechanically, without any sense of taste. His eyes seemed to have lost some of their colour. He moved more slowly and gave up his rugby training, saying that he didn't feel like it. A strange rash appeared on the side of his neck. He began to wheeze.

At first, the Brownes weren't too worried. All teenagers, after all, like to stay in bed. But as Jeremy's movements became increasingly listless, as he became quieter and more withdrawn, they decided to take him to see Dr Sheila McAllister at the local clinic for a quick check-up. Jeremy didn't argue. He had to wait at the clinic for an hour and a half before he was seen, but he found the time passed quickly enough, listening to music through his MP3 player, nodding his head in time to each track.

Finally, he was examined. Dr McAllister asked him if he was sleeping. Yes, certainly. He had no trouble getting to sleep. It was waking up that was the problem. Was he eating properly? His mother assured the doctor that Jeremy ate three proper meals a day, including breakfast, and that he always had plenty of fruit and vegetables, five portions daily just as the government recommended. The doctor took a blood sample. It did seem possible that Jeremy was anaemic. Or maybe there was something wrong with his thyroid gland. It was all very strange, but she was sure there was nothing serious to worry about. Generally speaking, Jeremy was in very good shape. This could all be down to a bout of flu. She told the Brownes to come back in two weeks if there was no change.

Jeremy thanked her and slipped his earplugs back in. Robbie Williams took him out of the surgery and back onto the street.

His situation got worse … much worse. Over the next few days, he became more and more listless. He took several days off school. Physically, he seemed to be shrivelling up. His cheeks, once so healthy and full of colour, were now sunken and pale. His eyes had lost their focus. Both his parents had stopped work to be with him, but he barely talked to them. Sometimes, it was as if he was far away.

He lay in his room for hours at a time, listening to the MP3 player, staring at the ceiling while he got thinner and thinner. He was still eating, but the food had no effect. His lips had begun to shrivel. His hair was turning grey.

More doctors and specialists began to appear. Blood and urine samples were taken. It was thought he might have a serious viral infection. The Brownes were asked if he had been offered drugs. Jeremy was taken into hospital, where he was scanned from head to foot. Various illnesses – diabetes, thyrotoxicosis, tuberculosis and brucellosis – were suggested. Jeremy was tested for all of them. He was found to have none. For the first time, the dreadful word "progeria" was uttered. Progeria, a genetic disorder, was also known as the ageing disease. It was very rare. There was no known cure. But Jeremy didn't hear any of it. He had gone rather deaf and he didn't care anyway. Long after his parents had gone, he lay in his bed in the children's ward, only partly aware of his surroundings, listening to his MP3 player which lay on the pillow beside him, the thick white cables snaking up to earplugs which seemed to be burrowing further and further into his head. *Tish-tata-tish-tata-tish* … the soft beat of the percussion whispered across the ward as the duty nurse walked quietly by.

Briefly, he was sent back home again. There was nothing the hospital could do for him, and so it had been decided to send him to a specialist neurological clinic on the south coast. Scampi the dog had already been taken away to live with relatives in Yorkshire. On Jeremy's last night in Elmsworth Avenue, Mr Demszky came to visit, bringing with him a box of Hungarian chocolates with pictures of folk dancers on the lid. It was only October and not yet cold, but he was wearing a black cashmere overcoat that reached all the way to the ground. His face was partially hidden by an old-fashioned floppy hat.

"How is Jeremy?" he asked, still standing on the doorstep. For once, Mrs Browne had not invited him in.

"He's not well," she said. The worry of the last weeks had changed her. She was short-tempered. She didn't want to see her neighbour and she didn't care if he knew it.

"There is no improvement?"

"No, Mr Demszky – and if you don't mind, I'd like to get back to him. We're leaving for Brighton tomorrow."

"I brought these…" He lifted the box.

"Jeremy isn't eating chocolates, thank you very much. We'll let you know if there's any news." She closed the door in his face.

Mothers can be irrational sometimes. It was only at that moment that Mrs Browne remembered that Jeremy had fallen ill shortly after he had first met Mr Demszky. And at the same moment, she found herself thinking about the MP3 player. Jeremy had always liked music, but since he had been given that machine he had become obsessed by it, listening to it twenty hours a day – at school, doing his homework, in the bath. Once, she'd actually torn it away to stop him listening to it during meals. Jeremy had screamed at her. She had never seen him like that before. She thought of the ugly slab of glass and plastic which was probably playing even now. It was almost as if…

It was almost as if it was sucking the life out of him.

A private ambulance came for Jeremy the next morning. He was able to walk out to it – but only just. His parents had to support him, one on each side. He was mumbling to himself, his eyes barely focused. He had lost a lot of his hair and his skin was grey and wrinkled. Some of his teeth had come loose. If any of the other residents of Elmsworth Avenue had been watching, they would have been shocked. He looked like a very old man.

He did not have the MP3 player with him.

At the last moment, acting on a whim, Mrs Browne had prised it out of his hand and she had left it in his room, on the table beside his bed. Jeremy had tried to complain, but the words barely came. He allowed himself to be led downstairs. Minutes later they were on their way to the North Circular Road, which would take them around London on their way to the south.

Half an hour later, Jákob Demszky entered the house.

By now he knew that the Brownes kept a spare key in the pot beside the front door, but even if it hadn't been there he would have found it simple to break in. He opened the door and went straight over to the stairs. He had only been in the house a few times, but he had no trouble finding his way to Jeremy's room as if he was being guided there by something inside. And indeed there it was, sitting where Mrs Browne had left it. Mr Demszky chuckled to himself – a strangely unpleasant sound. He reached out with a trembling hand and for a moment his fingers hovered over the MP3 player like a large bird about to land. Then he snatched it up and left.

He walked back to number 66 and went directly to his study, one of the rooms that Jeremy had never visited. Had the boy gone in there, he might have been surprised by some of the ornaments on display: the human skull on its pedestal, the black candles, squat and half-melted, the golden cross that stood, upside-down, on the mantelpiece. It might then have occurred to him to go onto the internet and look up the English for *boszorkánys* – or indeed for *tépőfarkas* or *gonoszul*. But alas it was far too late. Jeremy's eyesight had gone. It had failed long ago.

Mr Demszky set down the MP3 player and put on a pair of spectacles, which were actually inch-thick magnifying glasses. They would have turned even a full stop at the end of a sentence into the size of a button. Squinting through the lenses with his round, watery eyes, he produced a tiny screwdriver and ran it over the MP3 player until he found four equally tiny screws in the base. Taking enormous care he unscrewed them, and the secret panel that Jeremy had never noticed fell off in his hands. The inside of the MP3 player was exposed. There were no batteries … just a mass of circuits and a single switch turned to the left. Using the screwdriver, Mr Demszky slid the switch over to the right, into reverse, then screwed the panel back into place.

With a contented smile, he picked up the earplugs and pressed them in. It gave him extra pleasure to know that, until very recently, they had been in Jeremy's ears. Somehow it helped to connect the two of them. Mr Demszky did not like modern music. He turned on the MP3 player, rested his white hair against the back of his chair and began to listen to a symphonic poem by the Czech composer Antonin Dvořák. The music was dark and majestic. It flowed into him like a moonlit river and gratefully he absorbed it.

Maybe it was a trick of the light. Perhaps not. A few minutes later, his skin had regained some of its colour and his hair was a little less white.

Craig had wanted to fly. He had been given his wish...

POWER

ARTHUR AND ELIZABETH Reed had never expected to have children. Not to have any was something they had decided, almost from the moment they got married, and thirty years later they had no regrets. It wasn't that they disliked children. It was just that they preferred a quiet life, spending what little money they had on themselves or their friends.

When they met, Arthur was running the village post office which also sold sweets, stationery and other useful items to the inhabitants of Instow in Devonshire. He was a small, round-faced man who always seemed to be smiling and who knew all his customers by name. He lived in a very ordinary house at the end of a terrace, but with wonderful views of the sand dunes that rose up and down in yellow waves with the flat, blue sea on the other side.

One of his customers was Elizabeth Williams, a cheerful, attractive woman who worked in the local bakery, just a few metres down the road. Nobody was really surprised when the two of them announced their engagement. And it seemed that the whole of Instow turned out for their wedding. The bakers gave them a cake with pink and white icing, three tiers high. They took a week off for their honeymoon, which they spent in Greece, and when they came back, Mrs Reed, as she was now, sold her flat and moved into her husband's house.

Thirty years is a very long time to describe in a few sentences, but for the Reeds, time seemed to slip past without even being noticed. They had been in their late twenties when they met, but suddenly they were in their late fifties. Arthur's black hair had turned grey. He had to wear glasses to read. He found that he was forgetting where he had put things. And Elizabeth, after a series of minor illnesses, had become rather frail. When she went out walking, she carried a stick and could be seen waving it vengefully as if determined that the miles would not defeat her.

In a strange way, age suited them. In fact newcomers to the village could hardly imagine that they had ever been young. And they were still completely happy in each other's company, laughing at each other's jokes or enjoying long silences. They had just about enough money. Their house was cosy and just the right size. All in all, they had no complaints about the cards that life had dealt them. They were looking forward to a long and comfortable retirement.

As it happened, Elizabeth Reed had a younger sister called Janice. The two of them hadn't seen each other for many years, mainly because Janice lived in Manchester which was a long way away and, since her marriage, had become increasingly uncommunicative. From a note scribbled in a Christmas card, Elizabeth had learned that Janice had a son. Another brief letter had informed her that Janice had divorced. After that … nothing. Elizabeth had written several times but got no reply. She even wondered if her sister was still alive.

So she was very surprised to receive, one day, a telephone call from a man called Mr Norris who explained that he was a solicitor representing Janice. He wondered if the two of them could possibly meet. Elizabeth didn't want to travel up to Manchester but Mr Norris assured her that he could easily come to Instow – and so it was arranged.

The solicitor came down the following Wednesday afternoon. He was a thin, tired-looking man in a suit that seemed to have got quite badly crumpled on the train – or perhaps it had been like that when he put it on. He carried a battered leather briefcase which hung open to reveal a handful of legal documents, a newspaper and a half-eaten Kit Kat.

"It's very kind of you to see me, Mrs Reed," he began. He spoke slowly and without very much emotion. "You too, Mr Reed."

Arthur Reed had of course stayed in with his wife. The two of them were sitting side by side on the sofa, holding hands.

"May I begin by offering my condolences with regard to your sister."

Elizabeth had been fearing the worst, but even so the statement took her by surprise. "I didn't even know she was dead," she said.

"Then I must apologise for breaking the news to you in this manner. Yes. I'm afraid to say that Janice Carter passed away two weeks ago."

"Carter?"

"Her husband's name. She married a man called Kevin Carter in 1995. You never met him?" Elizabeth said nothing, so he went on. "They were married for ten years, but I'm afraid after that he left her."

"How did she die?" Elizabeth asked.

"She had a nervous breakdown." The solicitor took a breath. "She hadn't been well for a long time. And I'm sorry to have to tell you this, but in the end she took her own life. She jumped off a bridge into the River Irwell."

"Why would she do a thing like that?"

"She didn't leave a note."

Both Arthur and Elizabeth blinked in surprise.

"It's clear that you had little connection with your sister," Mr Norris went on. "Were you aware of her situation? I mean … her state of mind?"

Elizabeth shook her head, dumbfounded. "I feel very bad about it now," she said. "But Janice led her own life. She didn't even give me her telephone number and she hardly ever wrote."

"We have been trying to contact her ex-husband," Mr Norris went on. "But so far there's been no trace of him. We believe he emigrated to New Zealand after the divorce. It's possible he changed his name…"

"Why would he do that?"Arthur asked.

"I can't imagine."

"He didn't keep in contact with his son?"

"No. And I'm glad you asked that, Mr Reed, as that's very much the point of this visit. Craig is thirteen years old. He'd just started secondary school in Manchester when his mother did what she did. Right now he's being looked after by the local authorities. There are no relatives on his father's side of the family. And the only relatives we've managed to find on his mother's side…"

"…are Arthur and me." Elizabeth completed the sentence.

"So what will happen to him?" Arthur Reed asked. He could see the way this was going and there was a certain dread in his voice.

"Well, in normal circumstances, Craig would have to go into an orphanage," the solicitor replied. "But you are his uncle and his aunt. So we wondered if you might be interested in taking him in."

There was a long silence. Both the Reeds were thinking of many things, but mainly they were thinking of each other. They had lived together for a very long time and they had become used to being alone.

"Do you have a picture of Craig?" Elizabeth asked at length.

"As a matter of fact I do," Mr Norris replied. He opened his briefcase and took out a colour photograph about the size of a postcard. It showed a dark-haired boy in school uniform with a round face. He was rather plump and he had a crooked tie. Craig Carter wasn't smiling. In fact he wasn't even looking at the camera. Something appeared to have caught his attention at the edge of the frame and he seemed almost annoyed to be having his photograph taken.

"I won't pretend that Craig is an easy boy," Mr Norris said. "He hasn't done very well at school and his reports don't make entirely pleasant reading. But that said, he is only a boy. He has lost his mother in the most terrible circumstances and I feel certain that a complete change of scene is exactly what he needs. I'm sure you'd agree that anything would be better than an orphanage. On the other hand, the decision is entirely yours. You've obviously never met him and he doesn't know you exist. Everybody would understand if you chose to walk away."

But the truth was that Elizabeth and Arthur already knew what they had to do. How could they possibly walk away? It didn't matter that they knew nothing about this boy. He was family. He needed their help. There was really nothing more to be said.

That evening they discussed the entire business over a supper of cheese on toast and hot chocolate, which Elizabeth Reed carried in on a tray. Arthur noticed that she sat down a little more heavily than usual, resting her walking-stick against her chair. He could see that she was unhappy and guessed what she was going to say.

"Arthur," she said. "You and I have been together for many years and we never had children of our own. I suppose we didn't really want any. We were happy the way things were. And now, suddenly, this boy – this teenager – is being offered to us. If you don't want to take him in, I'll quite understand…"

"Of course we must take him in, old girl," Arthur replied. He had called her "old girl" even when Elizabeth had been young. "Flesh and blood and all that."

Elizabeth sighed. "He may not find it easy to adapt to our way of life," she said. "We're very quiet down here. This house is very small. You're too old to kick a football round and I'm too tired. He'll probably think we're a couple of old fossils."

"Still better than an orphanage," Arthur said. "And Instow is a lovely place. Maybe he'll enjoy it. Make friends. A new start."

"Poor Janice." Elizabeth shook her head. "What a terrible thing."

She telephoned Mr Norris the next day, and a week later the postman brought a stack of documents which they had to sign and return to the council offices. The next three weeks were spent preparing the house. Fortunately there was a spare bedroom on the second floor, and Arthur Reed got a local man in to redecorate. He had no real idea what a teenager would like, but guessed that it wouldn't be floral wallpaper and antique furniture. The room was painted white. A high bunk bed was brought in with a desk underneath. The curtains were replaced by blinds. At the end of it, the room looked very modern and new.

Craig Carter arrived a week later with a scowling social worker who introduced herself as Ms Naseby. Apparently, she hadn't enjoyed the train journey down from Manchester and needed two Anadin tablets with her cup of tea. Craig himself sat there with a blank expression on his face. Elizabeth and Arthur didn't have a chance to say anything to each other but their first impressions were not entirely favourable. It seemed unfair to judge the new arrival too quickly and yet…

Craig wasn't fat, exactly, but he was certainly out of shape. It was obvious that he had never taken much exercise and had eaten all the wrong food. He had poor skin and his hair, unbrushed, looked dull and limp. There was a triangular scar under one of his eyes and Ms Naseby explained that one of the other boys at his school had hit him with a brick. Craig shrugged when he heard this but didn't speak. He was wearing jeans and a T-shirt, both of which needed either washing or (Elizabeth thought) burning as they were dirty and full of holes. He didn't seem to have much interest in his new home or the people in it. His eyes, a muddy shade of brown, were utterly lifeless.

Ms Naseby was in a hurry to get back home. She gave the Reeds two telephone numbers – her own mobile and a general helpline – and left as soon as she could. She had come by taxi from the station and had asked the driver to wait outside. She ate two sandwiches, drank half a cup of tea and left – without, the Reeds noticed, saying goodbye to Craig.

The Reeds may have been old and old-fashioned, but they were not stupid people. They hadn't expected things to be easy, nor had they fooled themselves that Craig would accept them as his new foster parents just like that. But they were both pleasantly surprised by the way things went in the following weeks. Craig appeared to like his new room with its view over the sand dunes. He had never actually been to the seaside before and soon his room was full of shells and oddly shaped pieces of shingle that he had found on the beach. He was introduced to a new school in nearby Barnstaple, and although the teachers reported that he was way behind with his studies, they had every expectation that he would catch up. He enjoyed Elizabeth's cooking – she had, after all, spent years working in a bakery – and to begin with he even helped wash up.

Arthur Reed watched the new arrival warily. In fact, for the first time in their marriage there was a certain tension between him and Elizabeth. But it was a tension they both shared, a bit like sailors sensing a coming storm. The sun might still be shining, but they both knew that what had begun as a pleasant cruise might, at any time, become a howling nightmare with both of them forced to abandon ship.

Things went wrong one step at a time. It was as if Craig had been testing the ground, checking out the opposition before he showed himself in his true colours. And once he had the measure of the Reeds, the school, the neighbourhood … then it could begin.

He stopped making his bed. That was the first thing. Elizabeth had asked him to make his bed because she had a bad back and found it difficult to lift the mattress. But after two weeks, each day the bed remained unmade, the sheets crumpled, the pillows on the floor. Indeed, the whole room became increasingly untidy, with a strange, sour smell and clothes everywhere. Soon it no longer seemed to belong to the rest of the house.

Arthur and Elizabeth said nothing. After all, Craig was a teenager and all teenage bedrooms are a mess. Arthur had borrowed a copy of *Proper Parenting* from the library and the author advised him not to make an issue of it. "Young people need their own space," the book explained. "If they wish to live in conditions close to squalor, then they must be allowed to make that choice."

Then it was a question of food. Meals became increasingly difficult, as there were all sorts of things that Craig suddenly refused to eat – mainly vegetables and fruit. Elizabeth had thought he liked her home cooking, but at dinner-time he would push his plate away and slouch with his elbows on the table and a sullen look on his face. As a result, he began to lose weight. He didn't get thin. He just looked sick and lopsided. Once again, Arthur sought advice in *Proper Parenting*. "Many teenagers shy away from fresh food," it explained. "And the more you try to force it on them, the more they will resist. In extreme cases, it may be necessary to seek medical advice."

But this wasn't needed in Craig's case because quite soon he began putting on weight again. Even a place like Barnstaple had fast-food outlets and he had taken to visiting them after school, filling himself up on fish and chips, kebabs, burgers and take-away Chinese. The house was soon strewn with wrappers from chocolate biscuits, crisps and ice-creams.

And how had he got the money to pay for them? That was another worry. Arthur had given Craig a small allowance from the day he had arrived, but one Friday afternoon, he and Elizabeth were shocked to get a telephone call from the head teacher at St Edmund's in Barnstaple. It seemed that Craig had been bullying several of the smaller children, forcing them to give him their loose change or, even worse, to steal money from their parents and bring it to him at school.

That weekend, Arthur and Elizabeth sat Craig down in the living room and talked to him seriously about their life in Instow and how they had hoped he would make the effort to fit in. It was a mistake. For that was the weekend that war was declared.

"I know life hasn't been easy for you," Arthur was saying. "But your aunt and I were really hoping that this would be a new start…"

"I hate it here!" Craig cut in, and the awful emphasis that he put on the word "hate", the way he almost spat it out, shattered any remaining illusions the elderly couple might have had. "This is a poxy little house in a poxy little place and I wish I was back in Manchester."

"But if you were in Manchester, you'd be in an orphanage," Elizabeth faltered.

"At least I wouldn't be living with two wrinklies. There's nobody here my age. There's nobody to hang out or have fun with."

This wasn't actually true. There were plenty of teenagers in Instow, which, apart from anything else, had a fine sailing club. But by now they had decided to give Craig a wide berth.

"I'm doing the best I can," Elizabeth said.

"I don't like you," Craig replied. "And you smell."

"I really don't think you should talk to your aunt like that," Arthur muttered. Two pinpricks of deep red had appeared on his cheeks.

"I'll talk to her any way I like. What are you going to do about it?"

What Arthur Reed did was call Ms Naseby that same afternoon. And again the following Monday. In fact, he called her, and her helpline, several times before his call was finally answered. He was then passed from department to department, from social worker to social worker, but it seemed the bottom line was this: he and his wife had agreed to take Craig. It had been made perfectly clear to them that the child might take a while to adapt. But so far he hadn't set fire to the house

or committed any serious criminal act. So like it or not, they were stuck with him. The council had taken Craig off their books and they didn't want him back.

Arthur and Elizabeth had been happily married for more than thirty years. But now, for the first time, they found themselves torn apart.

Elizabeth felt dreadfully guilty. It was she who had opened their door to Craig Carter. She was the one who was related to him. And so all this worry and unhappiness had to be her fault. When Craig was arrested and cautioned for shoplifting, she blamed herself. When he was faced with expulsion from St Edmund's for threatening a teacher, she actually fell ill. She hadn't been exactly young when Craig arrived, but soon she was looking positively old. One night she slipped on a trainer that Craig had left on the stairs, fell down and fractured her hip. The neighbours wondered whether she would even survive.

Meanwhile, Arthur Reed retreated into himself. Once or twice he tried to have it out with his adopted nephew, but Craig simply sneered at him and walked out of the room without speaking. Arthur had noticed that a great many of his personal possessions had begun to vanish. In particular there was a handsome pair of silver cufflinks that Elizabeth had bought him for his fortieth birthday. One day, walking in Barnstaple, he noticed them in the window of a second-hand jewellery shop. A few days before, Craig had bought himself a new leather jacket. It didn't take very much to put two and two together. But there was nothing very much Arthur could do. A week later, thirty pounds disappeared from his wallet. Then his wallet went too. By this time, Craig had taken up smoking and the smell of burning tobacco wafted down from his bedroom, filling the entire house.

Not many people came to visit Arthur and Elizabeth any more. Once, they had been surrounded by friends, often giving lunches and tea parties. But more recently there had been several incidents. The sandwiches that had been found to contain a whole bottle of diarrhea tablets. The dog poo in the pockets of coats left hanging in the hall. The nails resting against the front tyres of cars parked outside. The lady who had brought her pet poodle and had gone into the kitchen only to find it shaved bald.

What were the Reeds to do?

They couldn't get rid of Craig. The authorities didn't want to know. Nor could they reason with him, for any attempt at discussion now ended with a barrage of foul language. Elizabeth was back from hospital but her limp was worse than ever and Arthur could only sit in pained silence, angry with himself, angry that he had so little control over his own life.

So they tried a new tactic. They couldn't fight with Craig, but perhaps they could win him over. If they tried to understand him, if they gave him what he wanted, he might even now turn a corner and accept his place as part of their family.

For his fourteenth birthday, they bought him designer jeans, a skateboard, an iPod and two new games for his laptop computer. In fact they gave him everything he had asked for, and for just a couple of days he seemed genuinely happy. But that all ended when Elizabeth made the mistake of serving cauliflower cheese for dinner. Craig hated cauliflower cheese, and by the end of the evening he was back to the scowling, swearing, bullying hulk they had so unfortunately inherited.

The next day was a Sunday. As usual, Arthur and Elizabeth went to church and then, because the weather was nice, for a walk along the beach. Returning home, as they approached the house they were surprised to see Craig sitting on a sand dune. His fingers were very stained and they could smell the smoke on his breath, so they guessed that he must have just stubbed out a cigarette. Even so, it was rare to find him out in the fresh air.

"Is everything all right?" Elizabeth asked. Whenever she spoke to Craig, she flinched, wondering what the answer would be.

"I want one of those," Craig replied.

Elizabeth turned and saw what he was looking at. Out on the sand was a man in his early twenties, with a power kite. The kite itself was huge, a brightly coloured, curving strip of silk or nylon, like a parachute cut in half, connected to two handles by a series of cables. It wasn't just the man flying the kite. The kite was flying him. He was running across the beach and leaping into the air, rising ten or twenty metres above the sand like a superhero. Elizabeth could see the muscles on his bare arms bulging as he fought to keep the kite under control. One moment he would be on the sand, the next his legs would be pedalling high above. When he came back down, he had to dig his heels in to stop himself being pulled away. He was fighting with the wind. His hair was streaming around him. He reminded Elizabeth of a cowboy trying to bring a rearing horse under control.

"It looks fun," Craig said.

"It certainly looks exciting," Elizabeth agreed. "But you've just had your birthday, Craig. And we got you everything you asked for."

"But I want a power kite," Craig whined.

"When I was a boy, 'I want' never got anything," Arthur remarked.

"When you were a boy, there were still dinosaurs," Craig responded. He looked at Elizabeth and there was a gleam of menace in his eyes, and not for the first time Elizabeth thought about her sister's death and began to understand perhaps why she had thrown herself off a bridge. "I want a kite," Craig said. "And if you don't get me one, you'll be sorry."

Elizabeth ignored the threat. She had noticed in the local toyshop earlier that week that even a small power kite would cost over a hundred pounds. More to the point, she had no doubt that even if she went out and bought the wretched kite, Craig would fly it a couple of times and then lose interest. After all, he hadn't even unwrapped the skateboard they had given him, even though he had nagged them just as much to buy one.

So she was very surprised when, lying next to her in bed that evening, Arthur disagreed with her.

"I think, all in all, it's a good idea," he said.

For a moment, Elizabeth didn't reply. Arthur didn't speak much these days. Since Craig had arrived, he seemed to have shrunk into himself to the extent that often she had no idea what he was thinking.

"The boy wants a kite. Let's get him one."

"But the money…" Elizabeth muttered.

"It might be worth it. Get him out in the fresh air…"

"It seems very wrong," Elizabeth countered. "We bought him all those presents for his birthday and he didn't so much as even thank us."

"We have to do the best we can for him," Arthur said. "After all, we said we'd look after him. I'll look into it tomorrow."

Elizabeth looked at her husband, lying in his pyjamas with his soft, blue-grey eyes and his white hair. There were hollows in his cheeks that she hadn't noticed before, and she realized that it had been a long time since she had seen him smile. She thought he was wrong about the power kite, but decided not to argue. After all, power was what this was all about. Craig had been living with them for only nine months but he had usurped all the power in the house. He was the one in control. Somehow, Arthur had been knocked off his perch. Arguing with him now would only make him feel all the worse.

Sadly, the decision to buy a kite only led

to further argument. Craig had already found a website that sold boards, kites and all sorts of accessories. It was as if he had known that Arthur and Elizabeth would cave in. But, as they soon discovered, power kites came in many shapes and sizes with prices that rose steeply to many hundreds of pounds. Craig had settled on a range called Laserblade. But the question was whether to go for the Laserblade 1.8 ("an ideal moderate-to-strong-wind buggy kite, perfect for those new to the sport") or the Laserblade 6.0 ("awesome power and brilliant rate of turn … for experienced kite flyers only").

Elizabeth remembered the man she had seen on the beach. A less demanding kite made obvious sense. Craig was short for his age … the number of cigarettes he smoked had seen to that. He really had no muscles at all. She could see him being pulled flat on his face by the first strong gust of wind, and after that the kite would be consigned to the rubbish bin. Anyway, there was the question of cost. The Laserblade 6.0 came in at an eye-watering £400.

This, of course, was the kite that Craig had set his heart on. And once again Elizabeth was completely astonished by Arthur's response. The price didn't seem to bother him at all.

"I'm not sure, Craig," he muttered, examining the picture on the computer screen. "I do wonder if it might not be a bit too big for you to handle."

"It's not too big. It's perfect."

"But suppose it pulls you over? You could get hurt."

Craig scowled. "If the wind's too strong, I'll let go." He shook his head as if he was having to explain himself to an idiot. "I'm not stupid, you know," he said. "I know how to fly these things."

"Well, you'll have to promise me you'll be careful. We don't want you in bed with a broken leg."

Craig said nothing – and two days later the new kite arrived in the post. By this time, Elizabeth was a little angry. She didn't say anything, but she hated seeing her husband give in to the spoiled, heartless brat that she now knew her nephew to be. Nor did she think that indulging Craig would help. She could already see that Craig would get as much out of them as he could and would still go on to demand more. She wished now that she had never opened her door to him. She wished the Manchester authorities had never found her.

"We'll take it up to Millbrook Common," Arthur said over breakfast. "There's plenty of room there and we can see if Craig can get it to fly."

"What about school?" Elizabeth asked.

"I wasn't at school yesterday or the day before," Craig reminded her.

This was something new. Craig had begun to play truant with increasing frequency. So far, nobody had complained. It was possible that the school simply preferred not having him there.

"There's a good stiff breeze today," Arthur muttered. "Good kite-flying weather…"

Millbrook Common was an open space between Instow and Barnstaple with farmland all around. It was certainly a good place to choose for a first flight. There would have been too many people on the beach, and anyway, with Craig skipping school, it was probably better to go somewhere more out of sight. The common was also high up, which meant that it was more open to the breeze. Arthur, Elizabeth and Craig took a bus up there after breakfast. Craig was carrying the kite. Elizabeth had the assembly instructions. Arthur sat with one hand in his pocket, lost in his own thoughts.

Eventually they found themselves on the edge of a wide, bumpy field with wild-looking grass that somehow looked hundreds of years old. The sea was far away and below them. Elizabeth drew her coat around her. It was the end of the summer and the leaves were already beginning to turn. She could feel a certain chill in the air and it seemed to her that there was much more of the breeze up here than there had been below. "I'm not so sure we should fly the kite here," she said. "Maybe the beach would be better after all."

"But we've come all the way up here now!" Craig complained.

"The boy's right," Arthur muttered. "We're here now, so we might as well give it a try."

"But Arthur, there's a lot of wind…"

"Craig has already said. If he feels he's losing control, all he has to do is let go." Arthur still had his hand in his pocket. "Come on!" he exclaimed. "Let's see if we can work out how to put this thing together."

It took them a long time. There were lots of different cables, struts to fit into place and complicated knots to tie. Eventually, they managed to construct the Laserblade, and Craig and Elizabeth held it down while Arthur unrolled the twenty-five-metre flying line. There were two handles at the end, one for each hand. He knelt down and examined them, running a finger along the tightly-woven material ("sleeved Dyneema, specially designed for a better grip").

When he was sure that everything was ready, he looked up. "All right!" he shouted. He had to raise his voice to make it heard above the wind. "Let's see if we can get flying."

Arthur and Craig swapped ends, passing each other in the middle of the field, and for a moment, if anyone had been watching, they could have been duellists, meeting at the appointed time. Craig reached the handles and picked them up, gripping them tightly in the palms of his hands. Elizabeth was trying to keep the kite steady, pressing it against the ground. The Laserblade was a brilliant red, blue and green and it was already trembling like a trapped butterfly.

Arthur joined her. "Are you all right?" he asked.

Elizabeth glanced at her husband. For the first time in thirty years, she realized that she had no idea what he was thinking. "I suppose so," she said.

"Don't be cross with me, old girl. I'm just trying to do what's best for Craig."

The two of them leaned down and picked up the kite. Twenty-five metres of cord hung across the jagged grass to the two handles and the boy at the other end. Suddenly he looked very small, compared with the enormous kite.

"Ready?" Arthur shouted.

"Let it go!" The boy's voice barely reached them. He could have been a mile away.

"Good luck!"

Arthur and Elizabeth pushed upwards at the same moment. In fact, they didn't need to do anything very much. The wind seized hold of the Laserblade and almost ripped it out of their hands. The kite flew up as if it had exploded out of the ground. It was a quite beautiful sight, the brand-new colours standing out against the grey, stormy sky. The two cables soared up with it.

Elizabeth gazed anxiously at the boy clinging on to the other end. "It's too strong for him," she muttered.

"He'll be fine," Arthur replied.

And for a few seconds, he was right. Craig dug his heels in and struggled to keep the kite under control, pulling first one cable, then the other. He was leaning backwards, shouting with pleasure, his fists pounding left and right as if were fighting an invisible enemy. The kite was now high above him, dancing around his head. All Craig had to do was harness its power. Then he would be able to run forward and jump. Briefly, he would fly – just like the man he had seen at the beach.

There was only one problem. The man on the beach had been flying power kites for many years, and his model had an aspect ratio of only 4.7 metres. In other words, it was one size smaller than Craig's, and – more to the point – the wind hadn't been so strong that day. That man had known what he was doing. Craig did not. He had barely read the instructions that came with the kite. Certainly, he had ignored the many warnings.

The first indication that something was wrong came when Craig's happy cries turned into a wail of dismay. He seemed to be punching harder and harder, his entire body jerking, like a puppet in the grip of a mad puppeteer. He was slamming his heels into the soft ground, trying to anchor himself, leaning ever further back, his arms stretched out high over his head.

"He's losing control!" Elizabeth gasped.

"No. He's having a high old time," Arthur retorted.

"We should do something!"

"If he's not happy, he can let go!"

In truth, there wasn't much they could have done anyway. Craig was twenty-five metres away from them, the same distance as the kite was above his head. He seemed to be swearing – at them or at the kite, they couldn't say. And suddenly his feet left the ground. Craig had wanted to fly. He had been given his wish.

But only for a few moments. He must have risen three or four metres into the air, jerked off the ground by the kite. Unfortunately, he had no control. He slammed down again.

"Bravo!" Arthur shouted.

Elizabeth turned to him. "Arthur, you don't understand!" she cried. "He's not having fun. He's completely out of control!"

"Nonsense!" Arthur waved a cheerful hand in Craig's direction. "It reminds me of when I was young. I always loved kites."

"But Craig isn't loving this one..." Elizabeth broke off as Craig was jerked into the air again. This time he hung there a little longer and landed even harder.

"Wonderful!" Arthur shouted.

"I think he's broken his ankle!" Elizabeth exclaimed.

It was true. Craig was howling. There had been a definite snap as he hit the ground, and his left foot seemed to be pointing the wrong way. He was trying to hold himself up on just one leg. He was screaming now but his words were incoherent, swept away by the wind which, if anything, seemed to have got stronger.

"You're right," Arthur muttered. "He's hurt himself." He put his hands up to his mouth, forming a sort of funnel. "Let go of the kite!" he shouted. "It doesn't matter if we lose it. Just let go!"

But Craig seemed grimly determined to hang on, despite his injury. Still screaming, he was suddenly thrown forward and then, before anyone could do anything, he was being dragged at about twenty miles per hour, face down across the field.

"Let go!" Elizabeth called out. "Let go! Let go!"

It was as if Craig hadn't heard her. He was like a prisoner being tortured on the rack, his arms stretching out in front of him, his legs – with one foot dangling horribly – behind. The two old people could only watch as he was pulled diagonally over the field, thistles and stinging nettles whipping into his face.

"Where is he going?" Elizabeth wailed.

"He won't get far," Arthur observed. "There's a fence ahead."

In fact there were two barbed-wire fences running parallel between the common land and the field below. Elizabeth was sure that Craig would get tangled up in the first of them and come to an abrupt, if painful, halt. But it seemed that the wind was playing tricks with him. At the last moment, it lifted the kite – which in turn yanked Craig off the ground.

For a couple of seconds he was standing on his own two feet. Then he ran straight into the first barbed wire fence.

Elizabeth and Arthur heard Craig scream as at least a dozen cruel metal spikes dug into his chest, belly and thighs. But at least he seemed to be pinned there. His ordeal was surely over.

"Let go of the kite!" Arthur yelled again.

But still Craig didn't listen. He stood there, clinging to the handles, looking both ridiculous and hideous, his white shirt covered with grass stains, his arms and face already covered in stings and blisters. One of his eyes was closed. There was blood trickling from a gash on his head.

"We'd better go and help him," Elizabeth said.

She was too late. A fresh blast of wind hit the kite, and Craig was dragged over the first barbed-wire fence and then the second. The Reeds could only watch, horrified, as his clothes were torn off him. It was impossible to imagine what the wretched boy must be feeling, but his screams echoed all the way down to the coast and several people, out walking their dogs, stopped and looked around them, wondering what could be making such a horrible noise.

Somehow, incredibly, Craig cleared the second fence. But he had left most of his clothes behind him. His jeans, in twenty pieces, hung in tatters on the spikes. His shirt was just a bundle of rags. Even his boxers had been dragged off as he was carried forward. Wearing only a single sock, he was dragged across the second field. And worse things were to come.

"Watch out for the cattle!" Arthur shouted.

Craig was in no state to watch out for anything. There were about half a dozen cows and a single bull in the field, and he only became aware of them as he was thrown once more onto his face, landing slap in the middle of a freshly-laid cowpat. Somehow he managed to stagger back to his feet. Now his entire body – his face, his chest, his thighs – was dripping with brown slime. And still the kite urged him on.

"Drop it!" Elizabeth screamed.

A couple of dog-walkers had reached the edge of the field and were watching with undisguised horror.

Craig still refused to save himself.

He was running, stumbling with his broken foot, straight towards the herd. The bull saw him coming and lowered its head, two huge horns twisting towards him. Almost gleefully, the kite dragged Craig towards it. Elizabeth closed her eyes. She heard Craig scream as he was gored. The animal twisted its head. Craig continued past.

"Why won't he let go of the kite?" she whimpered.

"It means too much to him," Arthur replied. "He must be afraid of losing it."

Craig was in the far distance now. He was getting smaller by the minute. All they could see were his back, his legs – now motionless – being dragged through the grass and his out-stretched arms still clinging to the handles.

"I don't like the look of those electricity pylons," Arthur murmured.

Elizabeth looked up just in time to see Craig leave the ground completely, rising ten or even twenty metres into the air. And, sure enough, there was a pylon directly in front of him, carrying high-voltage electricity down towards Instow. The boy was flying right into it. There was no way he could avoid it.

Craig was little more than a speck in the distance when he hit the wire. At once there was a tremendous fizz and the boy was burned to a frazzle. For perhaps five seconds, all that was left of him was a black silhouette, a sort of statue made of ash. Then that fell apart and finally the kite came free, leaping cheerfully to one side and disappearing off beyond the

trees. A shower of black dust tumbled back to the ground.

Of course there was an inquest. Arthur Reed was seriously reprimanded for buying a fourteen-year-old boy a kite that he couldn't possibly have controlled. But he was able to argue in court that he had suggested a smaller kite and Craig had refused to listen. His school teachers and some of the local shop-keepers also testified and the coroner had to agree that Craig had really brought his terri-ble end upon himself.

Most significantly, the dog-walkers and several other people who had been out on the common that day appeared as witnesses. They had all heard the Reeds urging the boy to let go of the kite. For some reason, he had refused to listen. His death, as prolonged and as pain-ful as it had been, was entirely his own fault.

Or so they all thought.

Perhaps it was just as well that none of them had been with Arthur Reed when he got home that day. He had been quite alone when he went upstairs to his bedroom, so nobody had seen him glance over his shoulder to make sure that Elizabeth was out of sight. And nobody knew anything about the tube of super glue that had been in his pocket when he took Craig out to fly the kite, and which had come out only once, when he had leaned down to examine the handles.

The tube of glue was still there but it was almost empty now.

Arthur dropped it into the drawer beside his bed, then went back downstairs to the kitchen where Elizabeth was waiting and made them both a nice cup of tea.

SEVEN CUTS

A NOTE FROM THE CHAIRMAN OF WALKER BOOKS

MY NAME IS DAVID LLOYD and it has been my privilege to be the Chairman of Walker Books for many years now. Although you may not know it, Walker is actually an independent company and specializes exclusively in books for young people. During my time here, my favourite titles have included the quite delightful stories of *Maisy the mouse*, *We're Going on a Bear Hunt* (which I have read a hundred times … it always makes me smile) and, of course, *Where's Wally?*, which has become an international sensation.

I do not like horror stories.

Don't get me wrong. I'm not some old fuddy-duddy who wants to protect children from the darker things in life. Nor do I mind violence (in moderation) in children's books. But I do sometimes think that writers can go too far and that there's really no point in producing a collection of stories that is going to give its readers horrible nightmares. At the end of the day, I am in charge of this company – and when mothers or teachers complain, I'm at the receiving end. In fact, for many years it was the policy at Walker Books not to publish horror stories at all.

After all, we've sold millions of copies of brightly-coloured picture books featuring flowers, fairies and children having fun and nothing horrible has ever happened in any of them. At the end of the day, I have to ask myself, who needs bloodshed and violence in the library when there is already so much of it out on the street?

So I was very concerned when Anthony Horowitz offered us a manuscript with the exceptionally offensive title *More Bloody Horowitz*. Encouraging children to swear is bad enough, but we had already turned down two other collections of horror stories, which were later published by someone else and are still in print today. I can't help but notice that J. K. Rowling has never found it necessary to indulge in this type of material – although, very sadly, we don't publish her.

But this time I had a problem.

Like it or not, Anthony has had a certain amount of success with his Alex Rider books, which are published by us. In fact, to be honest, our new, very smart reception area was entirely paid for with the proceeds from *Snakehead* alone. This has always been the problem with writers and publishers. At the beginning, before authors are well known, they're very easy to handle. They do what you tell them. But as they become more successful, they often become more demanding. We worry about offending them. Because the sad truth is that our profits depend on them.

Now, I'm not saying that Anthony has become big-headed or anything like that. But the point is, I was worried about upsetting him. At the same time, I was very reluctant to publish the collection that you now hold in your hand.

So why, you are asking, did I go ahead?

Well, after I'd read the manuscript I called Anthony's new editor, Jane Millitrant, into my office. Jane had only been with Walker for a few months after a very successful career with another publisher where one of the books she edited, *The Owl Magnet*, set in Belfast during the Troubles and featuring a disabled owl, deservedly won the Carnegie Award. She had also read the horror stories.

"What did you think of them?" I asked.

"I hated them," she said, with a shudder. "That one about the boy who was electrocuted in a field. Or that poor little girl who was eaten alive! I don't know how anybody could think these things up. And as for the story about Darren Shan being killed … he's quite a famous author! Would it even be legal to publish a story like that about him?"

"I agree," I said. "But what do you think we should do?"

Jane strummed her fingers nervously on my desk. She had very long fingers. In fact, she was an exceptionally tall woman with straight black hair that fell almost to her waist. She was married to the well-known food critic, Jasper Millitrant. The two of them had no children of their own. "I suppose we have no real choice," she muttered at length. "If we don't publish them somebody else probably will, and we'll not only lose the profit, we'll upset Anthony. But I really don't think we can let them go ahead as they are. We're going to have to make some cuts."

"What cuts do you think are needed?" I asked.

"I have them here." Jane opened her smart leather handbag and took out a sheet of paper. She unfolded it and set it in front of her. "There are seven cuts I have in mind," she went on. "These bits really are just too violent and too unpleasant. They'll have to go."

"May I see?"

She turned the piece of paper round and this is what I read:

— *BET YOUR LIFE: All the deaths in this horrible story are dwelt on in far too much detail. I think we need to cut the machine-gunning of Raife Plant and also the electrocution of Richard Verdi. Both made me feel sick!*

— *YOU HAVE ARRIVED: The severed limb on page 41 is almost certain to give young readers nightmares. The story will work just as well without it.*

— *THE COBRA: Charles wetting the bed on page 50. This is very distasteful. Is it really necessary?*

— ARE YOU SITTING COMFORTABLY?: Description of Dennis Taylor's eyeball exploding. This strikes me as highly unlikely and quite disgusting. Suggest we remove.

— POWER: Another electrocution, again described in far too much detail. We can certainly make a cut here. And why do we have to mention Craig losing his underpants on page 121? Completely out of place in a children's book!

I counted up the number of cuts that Jane was demanding. There were seven of them, just as she had said. I thought for a moment. "If we were able to persuade Anthony to make these cuts," I asked, "do you think we would be able to publish the book?"

Jane paused before speaking. I could see that she was unwilling to answer my question. "I suppose we could slip it out without anyone noticing," she admitted at length. "Perhaps if we published it just after an Alex Rider book … without advertising it or anything."

"But what if he refuses to make the cuts?"

"Then I think we'd be putting our reputation on the line. Honestly, David, I think it would be a mistake."

It was almost lunchtime. At Walker Books we have a rather delightful tradition. We all have lunch in the same canteen, down on the bottom floor, although, due to a strange design fault in the building, we have to go upstairs to get there. But today I had very little appetite. I thought I might walk down to the pub instead.

"Well, you'll have to go and talk to him," I decided.

Jane went pale – and she hadn't been what I would call deeply coloured to begin with. "I really would rather not," she said.

"Why is that?"

"Well … I know this is a dreadful thing to say. But…"

"Come on, Jane! Spit it out!" I didn't know whether to be annoyed or concerned.

"It's just that Anthony worries me. If you really want the truth, David, I sometimes wonder if he's all right in the head!"

This was news to me. I sat back in my chair, astonished.

Jane went on. "He sits on his own all day in that flat right next door to the Smithfield meat market. For what it's worth, it looks out over a crematorium. He has a human skull on his desk. He was given it when he was a boy. And there's a horrible spider in a glass case too. I know he can be very pleasant when he wants to be, but sometimes I look into his eyes and I see something strange." She took a deep breath. "Be honest. You've read these stories. Don't you think you'd have to be a little bit disturbed to write something like that?"

"Lots of authors write horror stories," I responded. "Look at Stephen King. And Darren Shan for that matter. Are you saying they're all barking mad?"

"No. I'm just saying they have a dark side, and with some of them you can't be sure where that dark side will lead them."

This was going nowhere. I decided to draw the meeting to a close. "Listen, Jane," I said. "All we're doing is asking Anthony to make seven cuts in a book that will be more than a hundred pages long. I can't see that he'll complain. I'm sure he'll be delighted that we're publishing the book at all. Particularly after we turned down the last two horror books."

"He's very precious about his work, David. You don't know him the way I do. His books are full of death. And you haven't spent hours with him, arguing…"

"Just see him and let me know how you get on." I got up and opened the door for her. "If there's any problem, we can think again."

Jane Millitrant went to see Anthony the following Tuesday. Her meeting was at 2.30 p.m.

She did not come in for work the next day.

The first I knew that something was wrong was when I got a telephone call from her husband, Jasper. Jane hadn't been home for forty-eight hours. Her parents (a charming couple with a home in Bridgwater) hadn't heard from her. Jasper had reported her as a missing person to the police.

I'm not quite sure what I thought about this. Editors, even the best ones, can be highly-strung people and I wondered if Jane hadn't simply taken herself off somewhere for a few days' rest. The last time I had seen her she had, after all, been in a state of nervous excitement. The police actually came round to Walker Books. I spoke to a nice Detective Superintendent and I was relieved that he didn't seem to be too worried. He was sure that Jane would turn up.

She did, two days later. Floating face down in the River Thames.

It seemed that she had been attacked by a maniac. The killer had taken a knife to her. She had been stabbed repeatedly and then thrown off Waterloo Bridge. I saw the headlines in the *Evening Standard* that night as, dazed and distressed, I made my way home:

CHILDREN'S EDITOR RECEIVES SEVEN CUTS

Seven cuts.

I'm sure it was just a coincidence. I mean, I wouldn't suggest that a bestselling author would descend into madness and murder to defend his work. Absolutely not. And I can promise you that Jane's unfortunate death played absolutely no part in my decision.

But in the end, I went ahead. I decided to let the stories go ahead exactly as Anthony had written them. I didn't want to upset him – that's all. Perfectly understandable.

I just hope you enjoyed them more than I did.

His books are full of death...

HORRORWORD ANSWERS

Across: 1. Black panther, 7. Grim Reaper, 8. Ogre, 10. Section, 13. Arsenic, 15. Run down, 16. Ghastly, 20. Obit, 21. Terrifying, 22. Invisible man

Down: 1. Blood and guts, 2. Cage, 3. Pain, 4. Nerve, 5. Heart, 6. Frankenstein, 9. Russia, 10. Scary, 11. Cain, 12. Intomb, 14. Nest, 17. Sator, 18. Lofts, 19. Limb, 20. Ogle